As If We Were
PREY

As If We Were PREY

STORIES BY MICHAEL DELP

Wayne State University Press
Detroit

14 13 12 11 10   5 4 3 2 1

Library of Congress Cataloging-in-Publication Data

Delp, Michael.
As if we were prey : stories / by Michael Delp.
p. cm. — (Made in Michigan writers series)
ISBN 978-0-8143-3477-5 (pbk. : alk. paper)
I. Title.
PS3554.E44447A8 2010
813'.54—dc22
2009045464

Designed and typeset by Maya Rhodes
Composed in Proforma and Brian Scratch

This one is for my dad, Wild Bill

Contents

Commandos

From up here in my room, when I look out across Orange Street with my dad's army surplus binoculars, I can look directly over at Darryl Hannenberg's house and see into his room. Right now he's pacing back and forth, and I can see his head and part of his shoulders over the cafe curtains hanging in his window. It's twilight, the time he always goes up there.

I've never been in his room. Who would want to go up there? He's the meanest kid in Greenville, and I have the bruises and scars to prove it. So does Richard Eherneman, next door, and his brother Nick, who has a small half-moon scar on his right shin where Hannenberg lashed him with a grass whip last summer. Other kids in the neighborhood have been knocked around, too. Believe me, he's drawn plenty of blood.

My parents have called over there a hundred times, I bet, and every time I hear Hannenberg's mother's voice apologizing through the earpiece, my dad shaking his head as he hangs up the phone. Last week Hannenberg threw a rock the size of a football into my side. I was out raking leaves, and before I knew it, he was on the attack, charging across the street toward me carrying the rock like he was carrying a bomb and then, Wham! I was out cold. All I could see when I came to were the bare branches of the oak tree in our front yard spread out above me. When I propped myself up to look around, Hannenberg was gone.

Tonight, almost dark, I'm watching him. I can see better if I stand up on a chair in the corner of my room and turn off the light. There's a poster of Hitler on his wall flanked by a Nazi flag, and a black swastika made out of shiny electrical tape, about three feet high. Nobody else but Eherneman knows what he's got up there. Not even my dad. I can't tell him about the Nazi stuff. He'd go berserk, call the cops and have the Chief, Hugh Corey, come over in a cruiser just to "dust him off," as my dad would say.

Last year, after Hannenberg's stepdad left for prison, I could hear him screaming. I watched from upstairs where I am now; Hannenberg smashing things all over his room. His mother was sitting on the front steps with her head in her hands; his sister was just walking around in their yard picking up leaves and twigs. "Loony-tunes" Eherneman calls her for wandering around like that all the time.

Tonight, Hannenberg is pacing like a wildcat. He's flailing his fists, jabbing at the air. I can see his lips moving. Every so often he stops in front of the Hitler poster and stands motionless, and then he's back at it, pacing, under the glare of one white bulb.

I'm watching him like I'd watch my neighbor, Patty Johnson, walk through the back yard to sun herself. I know Hannenberg's spied on her, too, and people have said they've seen him standing outside their windows at night. I'm really "zeroing in on him," as my dad would say, and when Hannenberg turns and looks out the window toward me, he raises his own binoculars my way.

For a brief instant we both look across the street at each other. Our eyes meet somewhere in the twilight haze, the two of us staring like sentinels toward enemy territory.

I drop down and then lift a corner of the curtain. He's still watching. He shuts off the light, and I huddle in the dark of my room, scared shitless that he'll charge across the street with a knife or that German bayonet he says he has hidden under his bed.

On the way to school the next morning he's down at

the end of Orange Street waiting, his arms folded, sitting on a fire hydrant. All of us—Eherneman, his younger brother, and Fred Baskerville, the biggest kid on the block, 220 in the eighth grade—are walking toward him in a herd. "He's nothing," Baskerville says. He can say that. Hannenberg stays away from Baskerville. Baskerville's dad, Orlow, is twice as big as his son and is known to have rock salt in his twelve-gauge. He sits on his porch like the neighborhood watchman, waiting for trouble. When Hannenberg sees us huddled together, he raises his hands to his eyes. He looks directly through the circles he's made of his thumbs and fingers and says, "You look into my room one more time with those stupid U.S. Army pieces of crap, and I'll make you eat 'em."

Even though I'm shaking, I don't let him see.

"Yeah, well, you do, and my dad will have you arrested," I say from behind Baskerville, my protection.

"Go to hell," he says.

"No, you go to hell," I say back.

"I been there already," he says, starting toward me. Everyone scatters except Baskerville, who makes a move to hit Hannenberg like a middle linebacker, but Hannenberg sidesteps him and starts for me. I race off through Hannenberg's sideyard, breaking through the bushes where Kumpula's yard backs up to Hannenberg's trash-burning barrel, and then I'm up Kumpula's steps, pounding on the door. But Hannenberg is right behind me. He stops at the bottom of the stairs, his chest heaving.

"Lucky, this time," Hannenberg says, when he sees Kumpula's face at the door, staring down at us. "Just watch your ass, otherwise I'll be feeding it to you."

Hannenberg's eyes are empty, colorless, "mean to the brain," as my dad says.

He moves away from me, pulls a Camel out of the front pocket of his leather jacket. He's not going to school, I know. He never does. He just follows along, a little out of range, to terrorize us. Sometimes he catches up just to breathe smoke into our faces. But today he just walks away, flipping me the bird over his shoulder.

I apologize to Mr. Kumpula, and then everyone comes out from hiding. We follow Baskerville to school, plotting about getting Hannenberg back for every punch and low blow, every time he hit us with stones or knocked us off our bikes. "I'd cut his nuts off," Baskerville says, "if I could catch him. Or I'd take him over to Fyan's junkyard and let him pet their German shepherd."

It's Eherneman who comes up with what he says is a "deadly" trick, something he saw in an Audie Murphy war movie, a wire strung at ankle height between two trees, the Germans tripping off land mines, their helmets flying toward the screen.

So, that night me and Eherneman are sitting in my room, sketching the whole plan out. "We're like football coaches. Or generals," he says. He draws my house first, and then the street, and then Hannenberg's and, directly behind it, Kumpula's place and his two prize pear trees, the ones in back of his garden. He draws in a big swastika in the square where Hannenberg's room is.

"Goddamn Kraut," he says.

"Kraut, what the heck is a Kraut?" I ask.

He won't tell me, so I know he doesn't know either. Then he blurts, "I know it's something about Nazis." Then he puts the pencil back on the plan and draws two X's, me and him.

"You're this X," he says, "right here," marking a spot just below Hannenberg's window.

"Yeah, right," I say, "why me? Why not you?"

"This is my Audie Murphy plan," Eherneman says. "Besides, he hates you more, and you're faster than me."

"No argument there, lard ass," I say.

Then Eherneman draws a dotted line from Hannenberg's to the trip wire, suspended between Kumpula's two prize pear trees.

"Right there's where we nail his ass," he says, drawing another dark X with the pencil.

Before I know it, we're shaking on the deal. "A pact," he says, and I say, "Deal," and just like that, we're in this together.

We watch from my bedroom window, waiting for his light to come on. But it stays dark up there. "Looks like it'll be a dry run tonight," he says. "He must be hanging out at the bowling alley."

"I don't know why," I say. "Nobody talks to him."

"That's why he goes," Ehernemen says, "just to look

mean and tough."

And I'm thinking of him hunched up against that green siding of the Greenville Lanes, no real dad to come down to pick him up. No friends. I'm thinking about his vacant eyes, the smoke of Camel straights rising up out of his sneer, one of his engineer's boots propped up against the wall—waiting like a bird of prey.

What I don't say is that I'm glad he's not at his house. I'm relieved that this is only for practice. I'm glad we don't do the stupidest thing I've ever heard of, which is to taunt Hannenberg into giving us more beatings.

"Commandos," Eherneman whispers on our way through the Kumpula's yard. Then we're tying the wire between the trees, and I keep remembering how Hannenberg's eyes look, cobra-like. We walk through Hannenberg's side yard and out in front of his house.

"Hannenberg, you Kraut!" I yell, launching a handful of acorns toward his dark window.

He's instantly off the porch, where he's been sitting in the dark all along.

"You little weasel!" he screams, running straight at me. Then I'm scrambling back toward the trip wire, shouting at Eherneman to run like hell, and I think I can feel Hannenberg's breath on my neck. When I turn to look back, I hit the wire, and Hannenberg is right on top of me, pounding and scratching with his nails.

"You little shit! You little shit!" he's screaming over and over, raging now, completely out of control. I hear

Kumpula's door slam, and then his spotlights come on, turning his pear trees, the entire backyard a brilliant white.

"You boys go home now!" I hear him shouting, and then he blasts both of us with water from his hose.

Hannenberg pulls up one last time, dripping wet. He's sitting on my chest, and the last thing I see is his fist slamming toward me.

The next morning, I wake up in my room, but it's hard to recognize anything. Eherneman is there. I can see my parents out in the hall, hear them whispering with the doctor. Eherneman bends down, "Nice one, Audie Murphy, nice going on a dry run. The wire was supposed to be for him, not you. You look like you got clotheslined by Nighttrain Lane," he says. You okay?"

"No," I say. "What about Hannenberg?"

"The cops came last night; your dad called. Hugh Corey was there again. But before he got here, Hannenberg got away, I guess, jumped on his stepdad's Harley and tore out of his garage. Don't worry. I took care of the wire."

"Holy shit," I say, thinking of how it must have sounded last night, Hannenberg's stepdad's bike roaring down Orange Street, the snarl of it bouncing off the oak trees all the way out of town.

I can hear my parents walking the doctor to the door. "Help me up," I say, and Eherneman lifts me up near the window.

"Gimme the glasses," I say, squinting through my one

good eye toward his house. It's quiet over there. I scan the porch, moving slowly up the columns toward Hannenberg's window. The light is still on, but as far as I can see, he's not there.

A week later, he's back. I don't know why, but he keeps his distance. Every night for two weeks, I look out across the street, but his room stays dark. I know he's probably up there, moving like a shadow. Now, on the way to school, Hannenberg still follows us, stationed on the sides of trees or leaning against telephone poles.

One night, later in the fall, when I happen to look over at Hannenberg's window, I see his light is back on. Only it's a dark blue light, not the bare bulb I'd always seen before. What I see through my binoculars I immediately wish I'd never seen.

Hannenberg is up there all right, but I'm frozen by what I see. I see a rope tied to a rafter, and I see him dangling, hanging there in his leather jacket. I stay low and silent in my room for a few minutes, as though there's a chance Hannenberg might have seen me. Then I drop my binoculars and call down to my dad.

Later, the three of us, my mom and dad and I, are watching the cops and an ambulance across the street from my bedroom window. They go upstairs, and I can see their flashlights pulsing around his room, two cops cutting him down. My Mom runs out of the room, her hands over her face. My dad just watches. Silent. I lie down on my bed and watch the ceiling, the flashing red lights from the ambulance dancing on the acoustical tiles, reminding me of an oil fire in Texas we talked about in school. How it burned for weeks, finally "consuming itself," Miss Burnes said, adding that "even Red Adair couldn't put it out." I listen to the street quieting down. I shake for a while, my fingers rubbing away the faint tinge of pain in my eyes.

"Go to sleep," my dad says. "Just go to sleep."

The next morning I wake up early, and the first thing I do is start watching again. For about an hour, there's nothing going on in Hannenberg's house. Every once in a while I can see someone walking past the front window. Then I see his mom and sister up in his room, taking down his flag, ripping the Hitler poster and the rest of his Nazi stuff off the walls. And I'm thinking that they can't ever get the hate out of the room, just like they'll never get the outline of that friction-tape swastika to disappear. Even new paint couldn't cover it up. Then his sister heads out the door, and the next thing I see is her walking toward my house.

Jesus, she's coming over here, I think. Only she stops at the curb on her side of the street and sits down.

She picks up an acorn and rolls it back and forth in her thumbs, then another and another until she has an entire pile cradled in her skirt.

"What the heck is she doing?" I say out loud.

All morning, whenever a car goes by, she rolls acorns into the street. I can hear the pop of each one. When she's done, she walks inside, leaving the street littered with the shells and the meat of acorns. Later, right after dinner, Hannenberg's sister and his mother burn his clothes, his leather jacket. His sister dumps a box of stuff into the fiery mouth of the barrel, and they stand back. I'm watching them holding each other, watching the flames rise toward the sky. And now I know just how mean he was. Meanest kid in Greenville. Mean enough to make his own mother and sister burn his stuff.

The next day I walk past the house on my way home to take a closer look. Hannenberg's sister is sitting on the porch, and I can see from where I'm looking that her arms are bruised, not freshly bruised, but they're that yellow color bruises turn a week or two after the blow. She's just looking at me. Neither one of us speaks. We just stare.

What I'd like to do is tell her that I knew how mean he was and that I saw him hit her when he dragged her up into his room, more than once. And I'd like to say, "I'm glad he's gone."

But I don't say anything. Instead, I walk across the street, the remnants of acorns popping under my shoes. Just before I fall asleep that night, I look at my binoculars lying on the shelf of my bookcase. I get up and take them down, burying them in my underwear drawer. I fall asleep thinking about all that hate lingering across the street and how the lenses of my binoculars spooked me, looking at me from the shelf like two dark eyes, the ends of cannons or tiny round windows in a house where nobody lives.

Traveling Einstein

If you happened to be sitting out in front of a gas station in a little town like Wolverine sipping a cold root beer in the heat, you most likely would have heard Art Bewley's '47 Dodge Power Wagon approach town about five minutes before you saw him. You'd hear the whine of a transmission, a truck with heavy-treaded tires shifting into low gear to climb the hill coming into town. Then you'd hear the announcement Art had rigged up on an old tape recorder blasting out the two loudspeakers he had wired to the front fenders: "Art Bewley, the Master of Minutiae, is headed into Wolverine. Ask him a question and win five bucks if he doesn't know the answer." The message was followed by Dave "Baby" Cortez playing "The Happy Organ," and then it would start all over again.

Art would pull in and take up residence in a lot near a gas station or a grocery store, and then he'd climb into the chicken-wire cage that took the place of the pickup bed, settle into his overstuffed chair, and wait for the questioners. After a crowd would gather, he'd shut the music down and lean forward in his chair.

"Ask me anything," he'd say, "any subject, any question, but just make it in English." He'd laugh. "Or if you don't know that," he'd continue, "you can ask in Swahili, the only other language I know."

If it was a town Art hadn't visited before, people would start out with stuff like, "What are you doing in that cage, mister?" or "What do you do for a living, mister?"

"Art's the name," he would always say, "and this is what I do. Minutiae, tiny details, ask me about the number of cilia inside the nostril of a gnat, and I'll tell you." Whenever anyone would bite on that one, Art would laugh and say, "Gnats don't have noses; therefore, they don't have nostrils."

Art Bewley lived on donations and the kindness of strangers. He looked like something out of the Dust Bowl, like a Dorothea Lange photograph come to life. He wore faded khakis and a gray fedora, and he always had the same suspenders on, a pair of leftovers from some fishing waders he'd found in his garage on the day he took off.

In some ways he was a refugee, a runaway from the teaching ranks who had cashed in his pension early, given the house to his nephew, and had simply "lit out for the Territory," as he liked to say. The Dodge was in mint condition ("cherry"), with its original steel (army green) and tires that would take him down any back road in Michigan. Part of the pickup bed was filled with crates of newspapers, *The New York Times* Sunday edition.

His questioners would always ask, "How'd you get so smart?" and he'd point to the boxes and say, "*New York Times*, Sunday edition. I don't like books, never read one. Never watch TV or listen to the radio. Just the *Times*. That's where I get my info, and I get some from people like you."

Today in Wolverine, Art was literally baking in the sun. Ninety degrees and almost that much humidity. He could hear flies buzzing around his head and Dave "Baby" Cortez slapping out "The Happy Organ" for what might have been the millionth time. His first "patron," as he liked to call them, was an elderly man who was on his way out to his car with a sack of groceries but had been transfixed by the banners and music; in fact, he had headed toward Art like he was magnetized.

No hello, no introduction. No "What are you doing in Wolverine?" Just a cold stare into Art's sweaty face. "What vegetable yields the most pounds of produce per acre?" the old man shouted into the cage.

"Cabbage," Art shot back, without a moment's hesitation.

The man leaned closer.

"What's a horned toad squirt from its eyes when it's mad?" he said.

"Blood," Art answered again, looking casually toward the sky.

"Well, I'll be damned," the old man said.

A crowd started to form around Art. He reached over and turned off the music and then stood up.

"You ask 'em and Art Bewley answers 'em. *No* question too difficult. Come on, dredge your minds, and if you get me, I'll give you five bucks."

In reality, Art had never lost. In five years he had never been stumped, never even threatened. He had no idea how he could carry so much useless information in his head, but every day at the end of his "sittings," as he called them, he could usually count on thirty or forty bucks, mostly in ones and fives. That was enough to buy gas and a little food, and left some to stow in the portable safe wired under the cab of the truck. He had no intention of doing this until he was feeble or, worse yet, reduced to straining to find even the easiest answers in a brain that might suddenly empty itself of everything that had carried him these last five years. He had a cash reserve of just over five thousand dollars saved up, and he was going to sit on it until he found someplace he liked enough to settle in.

A young boy in the crowd shouted out, "What's the rent for Boardwalk with a hotel?"

"$2,000."

"When do Bailey's Beads appear in the sky?" an old woman asked.

"During a total solar eclipse," Art whispered back, motioning his hand toward the sun. "And wouldn't it be nice if we could have one now to cool us off a bit?"

"What's my uncle's name?" a man cracked.

Those were the tough ones, the personal ones, but Art always deflected them.

"Keep it in the public realm," he'd say. "I know physics and philosophy, poker and pool, but I can't read your mind," he said.

The crowd laughed, and he could hear money dropping into the can near the driver's door.

"I'm not begging, folks," he said. "Just trying to make a living."

"What planet takes the longest to travel around the sun?" a younger man asked.

"Pluto," Art said. "Slow, ain't it?"

The man asked another. "What's the gestation period of an elephant?"

"Twenty-one months."

"What's the square root of 121?"

"Eleven," Art said.

Art loved the one-category types. His mind swelled and opened up, rolling with scientific facts as if they were millions of tiny bits of dust floating inside his head, one of them lighting up when someone asked a question.

"How many stars in Orion's Belt?"

"Three. You a scientist?" Art asked, laughing.

"No, just a teacher," the man said back.

"Me too," Art said. "Or, that is, I used to be. Got out when I couldn't look at the same faces day after day."

"What's the only venomous British snake?"

"Adder," Art countered, and he knew what was coming next, some off-category question, coming in like a high fastball after a series of sliders and slow curves.

"Bill Wambsganas?"

"Turned a one-man triple play in the 1920 World Series. Hah!" Art squealed.

"The guy's good, I've got to say," the man said, dropping in five bucks on his way past the can. "Oh, I'll be back tomorrow," he said.

"But I won't," Art answered back. "Got to move on north to the Sault. Once a year I hit the slots up there and give the Indians a little of my hard-earned money."

Art stood up from his chair, walked out of the cage, and sat in the front seat of the truck. He watched his audience disperse, headed for their cars, all of them going home. For Art it was another night in the cheapest motel he could find. He'd drive in, usually talk them down ten bucks, and take a hot shower. Then he would lie in bed, clip his little battery-operated fan to his headboard, and imagine watching the stars.

The next morning he'd be up early, looking for the smallest cafe in town, preferably one with dirty windows and lots of calendars on the wall, and he'd order eggs easy-over, a side of toast, and coffee with one ice cube. He'd sit near the window and look out at his truck. Once in a while a newspaper reporter would track him down, if the town was big enough for a paper, and he'd answer a few questions for free. He never told the truth about himself though. If you'd saved all the clippings from the last five years and tried to make a life out of them, you'd come up blank. In one, Art was a retiree from a construction company that built power dams in South America.

"I poured a million cubic feet of concrete a day," Art was quoted as saying. "I saw men fall into huge caissons, and we kept right on pouring. Almost every big dam in the lower Americas has men entombed in it," he'd said. In another version, he was on leave from Wayne Newton's Las Vegas Orchestra, or he was on a sabbatical from Slippery Rock College, writing a book on nematodes.

Each town heard a different story. A patchwork of lies and fantasies, Art called them. He likened himself to Bob Dylan, who never told the same thing twice about himself. "It's the mysteries," he would say when someone would ask what drove him to wander the country and answer questions.

"What's your IQ?" almost every reporter would ask.

"Forty-seven," Art would say.

"Forty-seven? But how can you know so much?"

"4,700," Art would correct them. "4,700 on the Stanford-Binet. Took it three times in a row and had the same score every time. 4,700." Then he'd laugh and slap a punch across the table. "Get the tab, would you?" he'd say. It worked every time.

The next day Art took his usual series of back roads, two-tracks, and detours to get to Levering. He followed the same drill every day. Drive in with a lot of noise. Set up "camp" and let them take their best shots. Sometimes the local police would ask to see his vendor's license.

"Ain't selling anything, just knowledge," he'd say. "But I got what you want." Then he'd produce the envelope with his name and title lettered across the top: *Art Bewley, Man of a Thousand Answers, Master of Minutiae.*

"Well, don't stay long," they would always say, and then they'd hang around and start asking questions with the crowd.

"Ah, a question, I believe, from one of Levering's finest," he'd say in his W. C. Fields voice.

"What did Richard Nixon have on his scalp?" the cop asked.

"A scar, left side, from forehead to neck," Art answered. "Lobotomy." The crowd laughed, but the cop set his jaw, another question forming behind his sunglasses.

"How many U.S. Marines raised the flag over Iwo Jima?"

"Six. Ira Hayes was the most famous. An alcoholic Indian," Art added, always conscious that to add even more information was the equivalent of teasing a bull in the ring.

"Okay, mister," the cop said, "Jim Bunning."

"Pitched a perfect game on June 21, 1964, bombed the Mets, eh?"

"Who beat Leonard in the Brawl in Montreal?"

"Roberto Duran." Art yawned.

"What's the last world of the Bible?"

"Amen." Art smiled.

"What two pins is the pocket between for a right-handed bowler?"

"The one and three," Art challenged, snaking his neck out at the cop and swinging his arm as though bowling. "Strike!" he shouted.

"Okay, one more, and I know you won't get this one," the cop said, his face red and contorted.

"How many stitches are there in the seams of a tennis ball?"

Art feigned confusion. He leaned forward and took the pose of the thinker. "Well . . . I'm not sure, but I think there are . . . NONE!" he shouted, jumping up from his chair.

The crowd howled, and Art could hear money plunking into the can like raindrops.

At the Satellite Drive-in, Art positioned himself on the bed so that he could see out the window and watch the traffic move north on old U.S. 27. Every five or ten minutes a car would pass, usually pulling a big Winnebago, headed for the Upper Peninsula, a place Art coveted more than he did the small towns of Northern Michigan. In the U.P., people waited for Art. He'd send postcards on ahead of his arrival urging people to study up and to get their money ready. He lay back on the two pillows and looked around his room.

Eight-by-eight, he counted on the white acoustical tiles. One drinking glass with a plastic cover on the sink. The shower was right next to the bed, and his pants were hanging by their suspenders from a hook on the opposite wall. He thought, if he wanted to, he could open the window directly in front of him and use the pants as a slingshot, maybe shoot tomatoes at passing cars.

When he woke it was past ten. He was missing two hours on the road and needed to get to Epoufette, a beautiful town with a white church on the northern shore of Lake Michigan. Last summer he had almost been stumped there.

"Here's a wrestling question for ya," a kid had shouted out, and before Art could tell him no TV questions, the kid nailed him.

"The Steiner Brothers, WWF, World Wrestling Federation, what's Rick's brother's name, and what's he do that makes him so mean?"

Art reeled. His brain caught on some jagged edge of information. He felt something tear loose in his head, hang there like a shred of skin or a flag whipping in the wind. Then he answered. He had no idea, truly had no inkling where the answer had come from. Perhaps, he thought later, he had happened past a TV in some restaurant, or he merely heard a TV in the background from another room. He had never seen the WWF, much less come across it in the *Times*.

"Bull . . . Bulldog," he said. "His name is Bulldog Steiner and he barks. Barks all the time, runs around the ring barking like a dog." Then he abruptly stopped the session and sat in his truck until the crowd went away. He watched them trailing off in the dust and waited for what seemed like hours for his heart to slow down, remembering that the answer had risen from deep in his limbic system, moving up through the blood and tissue of his brain like a bubble rising in maple syrup.

Today, he stopped the truck and went into the Epoufette Church like he always did, lighting a candle and saying a prayer for his mother, who had died his first summer out, and another for his father, dead before Art had turned five. He headed back to the truck, hit the play button on the tape deck, and tapped his fingers along with the bounce of the organ. Soon he recognized people. They dropped money into his can even before he took up his position in the cage.

"Nice to see you, Art," he could hear them saying. "We're ready for you this summer," Ace Buckner, the caption of the fishing boat, *Luny Tuna*, said. "Try this one," he said, knowing that Art knew he would only ask historical questions.

"What kind of animals was Napoleon afraid of?"

"Cats, Ace. Big cats, little cats, he shook in his tiny boots," Art said.

"All right, Art, who's the only president buried in Washington D.C.?"

"Easy, Ace, Woodrow Wilson."

Ace slumped off. "My two best," he said. "No use in hitting him with something easy. Somebody else try."

"I will," a soft voice said from way back beyond the ring of onlookers. "I have questions for this man."

The crowd parted. To hear Art tell it after it happened, he was mesmerized by her. She was thin and tall. To Art she looked like a perfect replica of Donna Reed in *It's a Wonderful Life*. Something inside him turned, as if all the tiny arrows Art had felt pointing in every which direction had suddenly and permanently turned and pointed in the same direction the first time he looked into her blue-flecked eyes.

Hers were literary questions, made elegant by the softness of her voice, the way she held her neck just so, and posed them rather than just spoke them. She held them out to him as though they were the most delicate birds, and Art took them just as carefully, marveling at the depth of her knowledge of literary trivia.

"Who was Sherlock Holmes' landlady?" she asked.

"Mrs. Hudson," Art said politely.

"What was Richard H. Dana's masterpiece?"

"*Two Years Before the Mast*," Art answered again.

He watched her bottom lip curl inward, her front tooth playing at its edge.

"What was the Great Gatsby's first name?"

"Jay," he said softly. "Not bad for never reading a book, eh?" he said.

She frowned. "I wouldn't be too proud of not reading, Mr. Bewley. Natty Bumppo?"

"*The Deerslayer.* You'd better switch categories, Miss," Art said.

"One more," she said.

"Who created *Yertle the Turtle*?"

"Dr. Seuss . . . and *The Cat in the Hat* and *Horton Hears a Who* and *How the Grinch Stole Christmas* and *Green Eggs and Ham*, among others."

"I thought you didn't read Mr. Bewley?" she said.

"Well, technically that's so, but I was read to incessantly by my mother," he said. "She read me everything from Mark Twain to Tolstoy."

"Well, I give," she said, passing the can and dropping in a ten-dollar bill.

"How about dinner?" he asked through the small wire squares of the cage.

"Sure, why not?" she said.

"Meet me at Grandma's Diner at six, then. I'll be the one in suspenders," he said, laughing.

He watched her cross the street and disappear around a corner.

At the restaurant she called him Arthur. He had

cleaned himself up, taken off his suspenders and fedora, and combed his hair, something he admitted to her he had not done in five years of traveling.

"Makes me look like Einstein, I think," he said.

"You look like the wind is in your hair all the time," she replied. She wanted to know things about him. At first he said, keep it public, but she persisted. He held his ground; she pressed further. Finally he laid out his life: his father's death, the upbringing in a small farm town near Grand Rapids. Teachers marveling in every grade at his ability to remember facts and numbers, batting averages and formulas. If he read it or saw it on the board, it was in his mind for good. He told her that he never remembered sifting through all the information in his head. In fact, he said it seemed more like dust to him, dust in some dark corner—deep and concentrated dust but dust nonethe-less.

She went back to her literary themes. "Tell me," she said, "What Shakespeare play begins, 'If music be the food of love, play on'?"

"*Twelfth Night*," he replied easily.

"What was Lady Chatterley's first name?" she asked, holding her hand up to her chin, staring directly into his eyes.

"Constance?"

"Did your mother read you that?"

"No, of course not," he said, embarrassed. "My college

roommate was reading parts of it out loud, and it just got stuck in here," he said, pointing to his skull.

"And tell me, Arthur, what letter was the *Scarlet Letter?*"

"*A,*" Arthur replied.

"For adulteress," she said. "Are you married?"

"I prefer to keep these questions public."

"Well, are you?"

"No."

"Why not?"

"Because I wanted to travel around for a while and see if someone could find something I didn't know."

"One more," she said, "then I have to be going home."

"Okay," he said, sure her face had grown even more Donna Reed–like, her skin luminous in the dim light of the cafe.

"What's the difference between what a man desires and what a woman desires?"

He was stunned. Dumbfounded. He sat back in his chair, leaned on two legs and stared at her.

"That's not a public question. You're a woman. How should I know what you think about desire?"

"Well, it's not necessarily a fact," she said. "At least it's not a fact like how far it is to the moon."

"240,000 miles," he blurted out.

"Or what suspect in Clue holds military rank," she continued.

"Colonel Mustard," he said.

"But it is a truly public question . . . At least you ought to know what a man desires. What does he desire, Arthur?" she asked, reaching for his hand.

He looked straight into her, and for the first time in five years, almost for the first time since the first grade, when his teacher had asked him what Archimedes had said in his bathtub, and Arthur had to admit he didn't know, because he didn't know who Archimedes was, he said, "I don't know."

The words came out as if they had been lodged for years in some kind of dungeon inside his body. He thought that if they had form they would have been tiny, eyeless white birds fluttering into the sun and then withering to the ground.

"I don't know. I just said *I don't know.* I don't know." His eyes opened wider.

"I'll tell you then," she said leaning closer to him across the table. "'A man desires the satisfaction of his desire; a woman desires the condition of desiring.' Pam Houston wrote that, and it's as true as any fact you know, Mr. Bewley, Master of Minutiae. I think you need to think on that one. I've been watching you for five years and have listened to every answer. I even followed you to Escanaba. I heard you stun the crowd with your answer that James Bond always used a Ronson, and that Stan Mott was the only man to drive a go-kart around the world. You truly are amazing, but I just proved you don't know everything.

Maybe you ought to keep me around, just in case there's something else you might not know."

When she stood up, Arthur stayed silent. He could not speak through his amazement and the blank freedom of not knowing. He had desires, it was true, and he wanted the satisfaction of his desires. He wanted her.

The rest is legend up north. They were married the next morning at the Epoufette Church, gleaming white in the slight mist that rolled in on a south wind off Lake Michigan.

"Do you take this woman to be your lawfully wedded wife, to honor and obey her?" he heard the minister ask. The question sounded like it was made entirely of steel and was forcing its way through years and years of newsprint, newsprint miles thick and weighing tons.

"Yes," he said, "yes, yes, yes. An easily answered question," he said.

They drove away in the Dodge Power Wagon. Sometimes she drove, and sometimes she rode. She learned to run the tape deck and would often nudge and urge the crowd to more difficult, two- and three-part questions.

Arthur never faltered, never missed; his life turned into something much larger that it had been. His last stop, somewhere north of Paradise, his last question before he retired and sent ten-years' worth of the *New York Times* Sunday edition flaming into the air, was at a roadside park, when a local Baptist preacher asked him what color Judas Iscariot's hair was.

"Red," Arthur said, as if it were as common an answer as "fork" or "spoon." *Red like fire*, Arthur was thinking, *red like the flames of the times, red like the fire inside my head right now, burning facts down to ash and char; red like the embers of useless ideas just before they flicker and die out.* And then, like a book, he simply closed his mind, took his wife and truck north to Marquette, and built a house where he would live out his days surrounded by art and books. It became a place where no questions were allowed, a place where he read without thinking, merely for pleasure, regarding facts and details as mere impediments to the simple pleasure of feeling his eyes crawl over the lines of ink on the pages he had kept out of his sight for so long. And when that seemed to empty his mind, he learned Braille, his fingers sliding up and down over the embossed dots of histories, dark books of poetry. Books and volumes that looked more like tiny raindrops had fallen on blank pages and left messages that soared through his head as if they had wings, never stopping to root themselves in memory.

The Trees Growing Up Around Us

I'm sitting outside of Willie Carter's house, or at least it's the house where he grew up. The place is across from Baldwin Heights Elementary, where both of us went to school. It's the house his dad, Zip Carter, built: a small white house in a small West Michigan town. My hometown. Nothing remarkable. Just a house across from a school.

If I stepped inside it, I imagine it would be just that easy to leave adulthood on the sill and become the child I was again. It's the kind of house that still looks the same on the outside, a place that inside might still smell like it did thirty years ago: the odor of slipcovers mixed with the scent of lily-of-the-valley perfume. The knickknacks are probably in their original places, along with the trophies and family portraits on the mantle.

"Willie Carter was a short kid," I tell my daughter, who is sitting next to me in the car. "He talked fast, always with a lot of spit in his mouth. He'd follow me around the playground and taunt me for wearing nylon windbreakers and pushing up the sleeves. He didn't like that, pushing up the sleeves. He said I was trying to look cool, like high school kids, and every day he'd tell me that, and every day I'd push them higher."

But Willie Carter and I were friends, kind of. We were friends in the way that only sixth grade boys can be friends. Surface friends, sports buddies. Teammates when we'd huddle in his yard. I'd call a down and out, and Willie Carter, looking like a fire hydrant that had just torn itself from the ground, would launch himself off the line and head in a crazy pattern for the lilac bush in the corner of his yard. I'd throw a spiral, perfect sometimes, and he'd throttle his short legs until he was under the ball, and he'd score almost every time.

We were buddies then, I tell my daughter. No high fives, or end-zone antics back then, just whooping and laughing and then the kickoff for another set of downs for the guys who were always on the other team: Dale Senn, Mike Blanding, Doug Martin, and a big kid who was as slow and unstoppable as God: Art Adkins, 180 pounds in the sixth grade. His team was always a man short. Adkins made up the difference.

I tell my daughter that tackling Art Adkins was like trying to stop a Cadillac, but I see she's only mildly interested. Why is that? In my imagination these friends loom, still young, playing out a string of summer days, our lives perfect, almost as if they were painted; they're still life landscapes able somehow to shift into action, and then fade back into the dying light of an August evening.

My daughter just nods, and I think I see part of myself in her face for a minute. Maybe the lips, the line of her cheek, and she asks me again about Carter's basement. The place I've told her about, almost a myth in our family.

I can still feel myself going down his stairs almost every recess. Our parents would write us passes and we'd leave school after eating and then head across the street. The same guys who played football after school went down into Willie Carter's basement to box during recess, where his dad had a workbench with every tool Sears sold: a radial arm saw, a table saw, and a joiner. He had all his tools in perfect rows hanging from sheets of brown pegboard, and a row of Gerber baby food jars, their lids nailed to a board, each one filled with a different size of nail or screw, each jar with a colored Dymo label marking its contents. There was something about those rows of tools, the saws, all of it motionless but capable of such power, just sitting there quietly in the dark. And I'd always make sure when I boxed that I could see them out of the corner of my eye.

The ring wasn't a ring, really, only a small space roped off in the corner, near the furnace. There were towels taped into the corners, for "protection" Carter said, and nearby what was really a workbench, the scorer's table. Willie Carter had nailed a bicycle bell underneath a tool calendar where a seminude woman turned her back, and every day he rang the bell with his thumb brushing her thighs to start each bout.

Carter's mom would follow us to the top of the stairs, offer a cookie or two, and we'd file down into the musty basement. The smell was a combination of wet drains and stacks of decaying periodicals—mostly *Popular Mechanics* and, hidden under a pile that we all knew about, a box of *Argosy* magazines and a few tattered issues of *Swank*, its pages blurred by our constant thumbing, the partial nudes blackened by our fingerprints.

Willie Carter would kneel down and take two sets of boxing gloves out of his dad's cabinet—a perfect piece of work with dovetail joints, the finish smooth as skin— and slip on a pair for himself and then challenge everyone in the room. Eventually one of us, usually me, would get pushed toward the dim corner and just start flailing. We'd cheer and shout, and in all those times we fought, I never heard Carter's mother say a word.

Even though she's only eight, my daughter knows boxing. We've watched every major fight since she was born:

Roberto Duran, Sugar Ray, Marvin Hagler. She's seen old films too: Floyd Patterson, Sonny Liston, the Bear. Even now, when I mention the Bear, she blows up her face and stalks out of corners in the house.

But she winces when I recount the details of my fights in Carter's basement. How, even after I took off my windbreaker, laced up the gloves around my skimpy wrists, and invoked whatever gods I thought might be hovering in the basement, he always beat the snot out of me. In the yard, playing football, Carter and I were on the same team, a quarterback and his favorite receiver. But under the single-bulb shop lights, suspended in their tiny cages, it was every man for himself. I imagined myself in the Friday Night Fights, some kind of crazed sixth-grade Marciano, pretending that Mel Allen was calling my rights and uppercuts and that I could lay Willie Carter out with one blistering haymaker, a yo-yo punch so hard he'd fall back onto the workbench and beg me to stop.

But I never did. Carter always won, every time, dancing and weaving as if he were some kind of miniature prototype for Ray "Boom-Boom" Mancini, and he hurt me bad once. To prove it, I show my daughter the mark over my left eye where Willie Carter opened up a slice over my eyebrow and I bled all the way to the hospital. Six stitches, I tell her. And I tell her the reason we're stopping by today on our way back up north, is to see how things turned out.

"Why did you go back and fight every day if you lost all the time?" she asks.

"Honor," I tell her, though I had little sense of that back then. And now, sitting in the car, both of us staring into the picture window of his old house, I know the real reason I fought had everything to do with vanity. I wanted to be cool, look cool, and pushing up my sleeves made a difference. Carter taunted and smashed that away every noon hour, and every day I tried to get it back. I fought for the same reason I rubbed O'Dell's Hair Trainer into my hair, then sculpted the front so it stuck straight up. I'd stand for an hour in front of the mirror to get my part just right: I wanted to be the one everyone looked at, the one who always stood out, and as long as Willie Carter was around and could snap my head back and mess up my hair, I was one notch below him. If I refused to fight, I was, in his words, a dweeb, relegated to playing hopscotch with people like Linda Belle Hoppough and Ella McConkey.

"Can't I just wait in the car?" my daughter asks.

But I coax, tell her it will be nothing physical. "No fights today." I wink, assuring myself that what is in the past can stay there, locked in its own kind of basement.

At the door, I let her ring the bell, and someone, someone very old and slightly bent, shuffles to the door. When she speaks to me through the screen, recognition comes like water seeping up out of the ground, the memory of a mother's voice. I explain who I am, and she smiles, slowly, just like she speaks, tells me Willie's moved out to the creek side of town. "A nice big house," she says.

And I ask, like a little boy, polite and almost shaking, if I can go down to the basement and just have a look. And she opens the door, lets us through, Jaime following me down to the last step. She looks around, taking it all in then runs back upstairs, for the cookies, I tell myself.

I reach to turn on the light. It's small, and I am shocked enough to lose my breath, to see that the tools are in their same spots, the saws, covered with dust, are just where I remember them. The same Craftsman screwdrivers hang on their same metal loops, the walls still covered in that pegboard that dads hung in garages and basements during the fifties to teach their sons where the tools went.

I open the cabinet, get on my knees and look for the gloves. Nothing. More dust, a couple of crumpled up Red Man packages. Back under the workbench there are still boxes of magazines, brittle now, and I reach, only for a moment, and shuffle nervously through them until I find the one we prized most: a decayed issue of *Modern Man* with half-nudes of Marilyn Monroe. I think I see remnants of our tracings all over her, smudge marks. But the paper has yellowed, her smile reduced to a faded red oval of lips. I stand where the old ring used to be, the cement floor still cracked in the same places, the lines converging in a pattern I thought back then looked like the tiny, twisted outline of a human body.

Just before I leave, I close my eyes, imagining myself

down there again, eleven years old, but it comes back differently. This time, I can hear young boys yelling my name instead of Carter's, and I see his face meeting the head of my gloved right perfectly, as if his face were some kind of target and he had stuck it out there just once, by mistake. I'm the winner this time, and he's holding his teeth, his mouth a fountain of blood and I've got my windbreaker on, the sleeves pushed up past my skinny biceps. I can see myself back there in my imagination, but I hear no words, only the silence of tools gathering dust moment by moment, and I hear the voice of my daughter upstairs answering all the obligatory questions.

On the way out of town, we stop at the Hi-Delight Drive-In; we wait outside for the carhops to take our order, but they don't come. Inside, they tell us that they haven't skated out to wait on customers for years. The place seems smaller, too. Everything's new and white, and my daughter orders a flavor of ice cream I've never heard of. We slip out the exit and head north along Main Street. I retell the stories of what it was like to grow up in a small town, where everyone knew everyone else. A place where you could drive the two-mile circuit up Washington Street and down Main, all night, every night for weeks.

I tell her about the life I lived, as if telling it could coax the ghosts out of old storefronts, places where I bought cherry cokes and fantasized my way into the arms of girls like Kathy Dolan and Linda Daniels. Their adolescent bodies still shimmer in front of me like apparitions.

We stop the car outside of Willie Carter's new house, and everything looks hazy. The sky and the air seem to have joined seamlessly in a cloud of August heat. He's got one of those mailboxes that is an exact replica of his house, and I stop to take a look. Every cut is perfect, and I'm sure Willie made it. I imagine him at the radial arm saw with his father hunched over him telling him to cut on the far side of the mark, just like my father taught me.

Suddenly I am back in my own basement, not Carter's, and I'm making a boat with my dad. It's 1965, and we've taken the plans for a Minimost hydroplane out of an old *Popular Mechanics*. I'm measuring and cutting, my dad right over me, and upstairs my mom is watching *The Edge of Night*, like she always does. My dad and I are gluing, and he's whispering about how true this boat is going to be, how it will look like a boat built by craftsmen.

I say out loud in the car, "Craftsmen . . . ," and my daughter shakes my arm and tells me she sees a puppy.

Coming around the corner of the garage, I see a boy, about Jaime's age, but a little bigger, chasing the puppy, while another dog is running right behind him. Jaime bolts from the car, and the dogs and the kids bound off into the backyard.

Then I see a guy who looks my age, a little fat guy, holding a rake, and I get out of the car. Willie Carter walks up as if out of the basement of my childhood and says in his clipped construction-worker voice, "Jeez, jeez, jeez . . .

Hey, good to see you. Come on in," he says.

Inside, his house looks like his parents' house, only newer and with fewer knickknacks. The wife is away for the weekend, he says, visiting friends in Detroit.

I look at Willie Carter now on the patio sipping a Pabst, and we talk about how old we both look, and our kids are out on the lawn chasing each other, with the dogs chasing them. In the air around his patio I smell wood; not firewood, but the scent of sawdust. And then I notice that everything is cut perfectly, each angle perfect; the corner joints are tight and flush, and even the table has been routered perfectly, a slight edge cut in its huge circular top, all the way around, and so I talk woodworking.

"Nice," I say, and Carter asks me if I remember the go-kart we put together to race down the Baldwin Street hill. We laugh, drink our beers, Carter reminding me that it was me who forgot to put steering on the kart. He shows me the scar on his upper lip from hitting Duane Young's porch, full speed, at the bottom of the hill. And so we talk scars, and I show him the scar he left me. The crescent shape just under my hairline. When he moves close to me, I think I see myself in his eyes, only we're eleven again, and he's weaving and bobbing toward me, that last punch he throws slamming home.

He takes me down into his workshop, shows me his tools. "No boxing gloves in this basement," he jokes. But I don't laugh with him, even though I'd like to, and just before I get ready to talk about why I came, I hear our kids yelling outside, up on the front lawn, and I hear the dogs growling. I hear frenzy, and both of us are up the stairs and into the yard, Carter right behind me, both of us huffing toward my daughter, who is lying faceup on the grass, the dog growling on her neck.

When Carter reaches to grab the dog's collar, I notice how strong his forearm still looks. Carter pulls the dog away, and as soon as he does, his son jumps on Jaime and begins to hit her arms, which have come up to protect her face. Carter pulls him off her by his shirt and hauls Jaime to her feet, holding one of them in each hand, the dogs yapping at his feet. Carter looks at me and then at them, and Jaime and his son are struggling against his hold and kicking at each other.

"What in the world is going on?" Carter asks sternly, and at the sound of his voice, the kids' bodies still for a moment. But before I can step in to make permanent this small peace, Carter lets them go, and Carter's son is suddenly running, and Jaime is running after him across the lawn toward the woods, the dogs barking and jumping at them as they go.

Carter and I are chasing after them now, but we don't reach them before my daughter leaps, catches Carter's boy and rolls him flat on his back and pins him down. She is punching him wildly in the chest and the arms and sometimes catching his face. And then, as I watch, Jaime stands up over Carter's son, her hands on her hips. She turns toward me, a certain shine in her eyes, and I finally find my voice. "What the hell are you doing?" I ask, incredulous.

"Getting Carter back, Dad," she says, "for all those times he beat you." And I see now that she's bleeding and that Carter's son is bleeding, too, and Carter and I just stare at each other in the light of an August afternoon, and I am suddenly aware of how old we are. How both of us look too fat, how violently our chests are heaving.

There is an instant in which it occurs to me that I could take him, but instead, we bring the kids together, both of us laughing a little, nervous and embarrassed laughs, and we make them shake hands.

"I told her about the boxing, you know, in your basement," I say lamely. "But I never thought . . . I never expected her . . ."

"No, no, he should know better," he says, shaking his son mildly by the neck.

I tell Jaime to apologize, and I apologize myself again and again, and Carter and his son do the same. Carter and I go back and forth like that for several minutes, apologizing, and by the time Jaime and I leave, Carter's son's lips have swollen, the dogs beside him panting in the heat.

On the way home, Jaime leans toward me. She rests her eight-year-old head on my shoulder. She's still mad. I can feel her heart running, but she nods off. I'm driving away from the place where I grew up. One more turn around my old block, past my old house. Past the apple tree where I built my first tree fort. Past my old school, and one last time by Willie Carter's old house.

Part of me wants to stay a couple of extra days, through the weekend, so that I can sit here on Monday afternoon and watch the groups of boys jostling and pushing each other, punching each other's arms. I pull over and look toward the small panes of glass in the room where I sat, thirty years ago, waiting for the noon bell, waiting to head for Carter's basement to duke it out one more time. Jaime stirs, tilts her head up toward me, and I brush the edge of her jaw with my finger. She settles deeper into my shoulder, half asleep, pushing up one sleeve of her jacket. I think I see a punch hit her face, a dream punch that lands solidly, tilts her head slightly. Then I watch her jaw set itself gain, ready for the next blow. I let it all flood back through me: the string of poundings I took from Carter, but more importantly, the way I used to live my life when I was a kid. How my father and I would head for the basement to build things out of wood and how comparatively gentle his taps felt against my jawline when I made a cut wrong or forgot to turn the saw off, the blade spinning against thin air.

I drive away, due north, my daughter asleep beside me. I leave behind a life that seemed to stalk me from the dark corners, ready to land a vicious uppercut at any time. I leave the ghosts of boys playing in their summer yards. I leave the boy I was, staring at the floor of a dark basement, his arms slack, the smell of blood and leather in his nostrils. Up ahead, in the last light of this day, the shadows from the trees stretch across the road, the car slicing easily through them, as if they were now nothing more than the absence of light.

We Are Living in the Future

Inky Sewell held his dip net close to the light, lifting and grunting under the weight of over two hundred smelt.

"Fucking-A! Look at that!" he shouted.

"Yeah," I said. "Yeah, lots of 'em. Let's get outta here before the law comes."

"No law around here. You know the DNR is short on manpower. Anyway, these smelt come up this river every spring, just for me and you. Now get the bucket ready, I got another dip comin'."

Inky Sewell. Look at him now, I was thinking, while I stared into a bucket of squirming fish. Inky Sewell was the best rovingback on the '69 Belding Redskins. He was All-State and all mouth, the people in town liked to say. But he was quick and fast and hit low and hard. What I saw standing waist deep in the river was low all right, but not fast any more. Well, the hands were fast, quick enough to sweep smelt up out of the swollen river, but Inky had put on the pounds. He looked like a woodchuck. His gut hung over his belt, and I could see different parts of his underwear poking out along the waistline of his pants. His camo duck-hunting hat was low over his eyes, and you could see the cold air of his breath sifting through a graying beard. I knew his eyes were in there somewhere, drifting around in almost synchronous orbits, the left one damaged by a BB gun pellet I managed to land in the fifth grade. From that day on I pledged, even with blood smeared in cuts on our arms, that I'd always keep both eyes on him. Over the years, I'd fallen short, moved away from town and managed only a few visits since his wedding.

I'd come up north for a smelt-dipping weekend after not having seen Sewell in two years. Right after I pulled in, we drank a couple of six packs like old times, and then Sewell was on the prowl in his basement looking for gear. Occasionally he'd holler upstairs to his wife: "Gail, where's my goddamn shorts?" or "Where's my goddamn socks?" or "Where's my goddamn anything?" He punctuated everything with swearing, just like he had in high school.

Back then he said he did it for emphasis, thinking that a Methodist preacher's son might get more attention if he swore and drank. He always carried a pocket Bible with him, but he could swear better than anybody's uncle. Once I saw him haul out the Bible at the bowling alley. Elwood Hole, the kid who was always the disc jockey at the school dances, was giving Sewell some shit homo ball release. I'll never forget watching Sewell put the Bible on the ball rack.

"What's that for," Hole shouted over, "luck?"

"Don't need it, you silly shit. It's for prayer power." Sewell said.

"Prayer power," Hole said, laughing.

"Fucking right, dimwit," Sewell shot back. "A buck a pin."

"You're on," Hole said back. Then Sewell proceeded to reel off ten straight strikes.

What Hole didn't know was that Jimmy Ballard was setting pins that night and was using his special "rocker bottom" pins on Sewell's lane. Even a gutter ball would have sent them flying. That night we drank beer using Hole's losings until we thought we'd explode, and then we threw up all over the football field, laughing our asses off over every Hole joke we could come up with.

"It was the Bible that got him most," Sewell was laughing. "Mr. Hole to the phone," Sewell sang, mimicking the voice of the desk man at the Whiting hotel downtown, where Elwood played pool on Saturday nights. We'd use the pay phone around the corner and have Elwood summoned from his game. Then we'd hide and watch him shuffle from the table to the desk phone.

He'd say hello into the receiver a dozen times. "Who was it?" he'd ask, every single time.

And every time, the clerk would say it was a woman, "Or maybe a girl." Sewell and I would make up different names. Once, "She said her name was Finger. Julie Finger. She said she was looking for a Hole, a Mr. Hole." Then Elwood would stomp off, and Sewell and I would be holding our sides and howling all the way down the street.

In the basement of Sewell's house, as he yelled up to his wife, I was thinking that he sure seemed helpless. I was thinking how easy it is to start out so promising and then end up in a slump. But Sewell had done all right for a while.

His first job in Traverse City had been with Schmuckal Oil on a delivery route. "Hot shit," he said to me when they made the offer, "I'm headed north." But that never panned out, as they say, and soon enough Sewell's wife was working at Meijer's bakery on the night shift, and Sewell was dipping minnows for local bait shops, mostly small shiners at two cents apiece and a nickel for the larger grays most guys use for pike up here. I teased him plenty when he started to drink too much beer and gain weight, his T-shirts bulging over his man-boobs, easy targets for titty twisters. But after a while, I just didn't have the heart once he told me how he'd stand under the bridge for hours, sometimes stopping to eat a sandwich and drink a beer, his back against the rough cement of the footings. "Like a troll," he'd say. "I live under the bridges all over the county, like a fuckin' troll."

"I got a million of 'em," he said, holding the net up to my tiny penlight. "Jeez," he said, "Don't shine that thing out here ... Gimme a beer, would ya?" He poked his hands down into the net and stirred the smelt like they were some kind of broth in the river. He looked like a mad chemist or some ancient priest, maybe, lifted up out of the dark ages and plopped into the river. Now he was trying to stir himself back to what he once was.

When we got the smelt home, Sewell pulled out a bucket and two pairs of scissors, and for the next two hours we sat in the kitchen and stuffed fifty at a time into plastic bags, first snipping off their tiny heads and dropping them into the bucket. Most of them were headed for the freezer, for eating in July, batter dipped, with lots of cold beer. I thought of how we'd eat them on the Fourth: bones and all, tail first, eating until we could barely walk.

"Good for eating later, but we'll have some of these right now," he said, hollering for Gail to turn on the stove.

"She's awful good to me," he said, almost starting to cry, probably a result of drinking so many beers, or maybe it was the accumulation of hours and days spent under bridges, his future lost under there with him, as though he were stumbling around inside a tunnel without an exit.

49

"Ever since I lost the Schmuckal's job, she's been do-ing everything she can to make me happy . . . but you know as well as I do dipping bait for a living ain't exactly the cat's ass."

Gail walked in and handed us each a Stroh's and then took a hundred or so smelt from the bucket and walked back into the kitchen. She still looked good to me, just like she had in high school. A little wider I thought, but she still had that perfect curve around her waist, so that her hips stuck out just right. I doubted that Sewell even paid much attention to her; he had spent most of his adult life "sniffing skirts," as he put it.

He was always chasing as many women as he could, even after high school and on into his marriage. To him Gail must have been just a spectator on the sidelines when he ran back interceptions or knocked out quarter-backs, like he did to Al Baker in the conference champi-onship game. Sewell sent Baker to the hospital for a week with a concussion.

The three of us sat at the kitchen table and ate batter-dipped smelt, drinking beer and listening to some old eight-track tapes from the seventies. Sewell was oiling himself up pretty good, when he suddenly stood straight up and looked into my eyes.

"I know about you and Gail," he said. "Under that god-damn float in 1968. Just last week we had a fight, and she let the beans spill. I never thought you'd cross me like that!" he screamed.

"Cross you?" I yelled back. "You were out dinging Jane Rasmussen or somebody else that night! I was just trying to give Gail a little comfort, that's all."

"Comfort, my ass," he shot back. And before I knew it, he was on top of me, flailing away at my head. I could feel the fish heads spilling out of the pail, both of us slipping around in fish heads and blood. Gail was yelling at us to stop, but we kept swinging at each other. Then Sewell stood up over me and spit in my face.

"See you later, you sons of bitches," he said to both of us and headed out the door.

Gail was standing next to me, her chest heaving, out of breath.

"I knew I shouldn't have told him. I thought it was innocent enough. Jeez, we were just kids," she said, looking at me.

Maybe it was the glance that did it, those same green eyes with tiny flecks of blue in them. She looked twenty years younger. It was 1968 all over again. I leaned closer to her and the smell coming off her skin almost knocked me over. She smelled exactly the way she had smelled that night . . . a mixture of sweat and Jasmine Musk, her favorite perfume.

I imagined sliding my hands around her waist exactly as I had after we'd crawled into the sophomore float, a huge replica of an Indian brave's head, decorated with red crepe paper. And, when it started to rain, the water dripped down our heads and turned our hair and faces blood red. I wanted her right there in the kitchen, fish guts and all, even if Sewell was on the prowl somewhere around the yard.

"I can't," she whispered. "I just can't."

"I know . . . I can't either, but I sure would like to," I said, just reaching out to graze her arm.

"Sewell would kill us both," she said. "We better go find him."

"Where?" I asked. "He just stormed out, he could be anywhere."

"Nah," she said. "When he's upset he walks up the road to the bridge and just sits under there. Sometimes he stays there all night drinking Jack Daniels, and sometimes he just dips minnows and lets them go. . . . You know, losing his job is killing him, and this bait-gathering stuff is no way to make a living."

"Yeah," I said. "I suspected as much, but let's just find him before he gets madder."

We headed outside and looked up the street. The bridge was spooky looking, covered in mist, the only light coming from a vapor lamp in a nearby yard. We hopped in the truck and drove up to the bridge, and then stopped at the railing and stood, listening. We could hear him underneath us, half humming and half whispering an old John Prine tune we both liked, "The Speed of the Sound of Loneliness." Under his breath I could hear Sewell, "You come home straight and you come home curly . . ."

When he got to the right line, I chimed in, "You're out

there running just to be on the run." I could hear him laughing a little, and then he sang back, louder, his voice full of whiskey, about his feverish heart and his jealous mind.

"Sewell!" I yelled. "Get yer ass back up here."

"Nope!" he shouted back. "I got thinking to do. Just go away, and I'll see you in the morning."

"It's no use now," Gail said. "I've been on this bridge plenty of times, and when he gets this way, you just got to let him go."

Both of us heard the splash at the same time, and then Sewell was shouting and sputtering.

"Help me!" he screamed. "For Christ's sake help me! Get down here."

We ran around the abutments and hunched under the bridge. I could see the faint outline of Sewell's head in the water. He was flailing his arms, screaming.

"My leg's caught in a goddamn beaver trap!" he said. "Get me outta here!"

I jumped in and held his head above the water. "Just pull it loose," he said, "The security chain must be caught on a rock or some goddamn thing. Get me outta here."

He was crying, blubbering like a little kid. I'd never seen him that way. Back in Belding, he was always the tough guy, the one who rode around in his dad's Pontiac Lemans with the vinyl top and the automatic on the floor. He drove that car like he was the King Shit of Turd Island, and I guess all of us thought he was. But now, he was resting in my arms. Gail was right next to me. She ran her hands over his face.

"You'll be all right soon enough, honey," she said.

"Yeah, well I want to be all right now," he said.

I had Gail hold him and then dove underwater, and in the thin light I saw his leg trailing a wisp of blood, and farther down, the metal trap. When I popped up, he was still shouting. I half thought of leaving him there until the ice came in, maybe letting him freeze, knowing what I might have if he wasn't around. But I went back down instead, and I grabbed the jaws of the trap with both hands and pulled them apart. He came out of the water like a wet towel, limp and cold, as if he had been showering too long in the locker room and had run out of warm water, caved in by the last in a string of pulverizing losses. He just lay back on the gravelly shore and stretched out his arms. "I give," he said. "I give, I give, goddammit."

He smelled like fish. His face was puffed and white, his body close to hypothermia. Together Gail and I lifted him up onto the road and half-carried him to the truck. He was too stiff to fit into the cab so we spread him out in the bed of the pickup and headed back to his house.

That's where I last saw him, lying on his couch with a hundred blankets over him, hot water bottles under his feet. I'd have given anything to be him when I left, huddled there under all those blankets waiting for Gail to slip out of her jeans and her underwear to slide in next to me and give me some warmth.

I imagined them like that all the way home. Gail snuggled tight against his entire body. Imagined the smell of her rising as she gave away heat, and Sewell there devouring it. How it must have felt like steam coming into his nostrils, some kind of wonderful mist welling up out of her lungs, out of her pores, until it filled him with the sweet scent of perfume.

When I got home, I hung my varsity jacket in the garage, right next to the two trophies we'd won in football. State champs two years in a row. I wanted my own wife back, wanted the garage to suddenly lift away, and I'd find myself back at Rigdon's Field, me and Sewell drifting toward the line of scrimmage, red-dogging on a quarterback, his eyes starting to roll back in his head. Instead, I stumbled into the kitchen, road tired, a little shaky from too much Stroh's over the weekend. I looked in the mirror over the bathroom sink and wanted to cry, thinking about Gail, thinking about that goddamn float, about how, Sewell, lying there under the bridge, shouting, "I give, I give, I give!" had almost looked like he'd been crucified. When I raised my hand to my face just to make sure it was still my face, I caught the scent of beer, the thick smell of fish, and the ever so slight odor of jasmine.

Therapy

We'd been out road hunting. Cofer drove, and I watched for partridge in the trees. When we saw any, we'd pull the truck over about a hundred yards from where we spotted them and then sneak up through the woods and open fire.

Maybe that's what got Cofer going, driving for an hour without seeing a single bird, but from the way he looked when he picked me up, I could tell something was wrong. His face had the look of a guy who had been crawling along a high ledge. He looked white and exhausted.

"Bleak," he said when I asked him how he was when I got in, and bleak he stayed.

I tried all sorts of things to cheer him up. I told the same kinds of farting jokes I always told when we rode in the truck. I knew Marlene had been on him the whole week about getting a job. Last weekend she'd made him drive all the way to town for a box of Ding Dongs. The only reason I know is that I'm Cofer's only friend, and so when he goes, I go. Whether it's Ding Dongs or Kotex, I get the nod. Shotgun is where I ride.

And what drives Cofer nuts most is fiddling with the radio dial. So, last weekend, on the Ding Dong trip, I fiddled like crazy: up and down, over and over. He hated it when I did it too fast. "Christ," he'd say. "Move it slow, don't tax nothing."

That was Cofer's whole philosophy of life: don't tax nothing. Take everything slow. Real slow. But I fiddled anyway, short bursts of country-western tunes, and then I'd switch to that classical station both of us hated. He'd swerve the truck and say, every time, "You dickhead," and switch it back to the station that played only oldies.

I suspected he was out of sorts when he picked me up today for the pat patrol, which is the name he gave it, not me. When he said it, "pat patrol," he made a sound like a little kid playing with a toy police car, his finger whirling in the air.

The radio was off when I got in, and he was sort of half humming something by the Righteous Brothers. When I asked him about not having the radio on after he said he was so bleak, all he could do was drop into low gear and take off. "I'm telling you, this time, I'm really telling you," he muttered, the truck inching out of my driveway.

After several miles of listening to him hum, I couldn't stand it any longer. "It's Marlene again, ain't it?" I said.

And he said, almost as if a ghost was talking, "Yeah."

"What's wrong now?" I asked.

"Her mother's coming to live with us next week for good. And I'm leaving. Just told her today. Check the bed," he said, pointing with his thumb behind the cab.

When I looked through the window all I could see was piles of clothes shifting in the wind, some old Playboys flapping around, an eight-track stereo, and a pair of waders. Just like it looked the last time he threatened to move out, only this time he said he was serious.

"No kidding," I said, playing along.

"No shit, Dick Tracy," he mumbled back. Then I saw them through the flecks of snow on the windshield, a whole covey of partridges sitting in a maple like ornaments on a Christmas tree. I motioned toward the sky, and Cofer slowed down, looked up through the window, and it was then I could see he was crying.

When he knew that I knew, he looked directly at me and started shaking. "You gotta help me," he said. He knew, because I was truly his only friend, that I had watched for months as he inched along that narrow ledge of our lives when the first and last impulse is to just let yourself go; he knew I would have to help. I was bound to help, no matter how stupid or ill-conceived the idea was. Even if it was dangerous, Cofer knew I'd be there.

"Pull off," I said. And Cofer aimed the truck over toward the shoulder, reaching under the seat as he slid out. "Don't forget your gun," I said.

"Don't need it," he whispered back, opening the hood of the truck.

He had a set of jumper cables in his hand. When I got out and stood next to him, he started to hook them up to the car battery, positive to positive, negative to negative. "Remember," he said, "You're helping," motioning me closer. When I got next to him, I could see how red his eyes really were, the pupils dark and tiny, like the door-knobs to cheap hotel rooms where strangers slept in the cold.

In half a voice, he told me to hold the loose negative clamp while he hooked the positive cable to his left ear, no sign in his face of pain, only pure vacancy.

"What in the fuck are you doing?" I shouted.

"Just help!" he shouted back.

"But Christ, Cofer, it can't be bad enough to kill yourself," I said.

"Nobody's dying. Now help," he said, forcing the negative clamp into my hand, motioning for me to touch the positive clamp to his leg.

I waited for a second or two for the joke to show itself, the way it always did when he was up to something stupid. He had done something like this before: Once with his hat full of lighter fluid at the Hofbrau bar, he had threatened, in despair again, to light it on fire and put it on. Only then, he lit the match, and just before he dropped it into the hat, he put the flame inside his mouth and snuffed it out with his breath, laughing until he fell off his chair.

I shook him just once.

"Do it," he said. "This ain't like that hat trick at the bar," as though he'd read my mind.

"Jesus, you are serious," I said, noticing now some kind of odd resolve that had seemed to reshape the bones of his face. He looked quiet, still, stalled, like some bird of prey about to drop down on a piece of roadkill.

He reached for my hand and slid it up his pant leg, the other clamp pinching the grey-white skin of his calf. Then he stood upright and took off his glove, touching his wedding band to the battery terminal. A blue arc lifted, almost in slow motion from the battery, traveled up his left arm and then his whole body shook, only for a second or two. He fell back into the snow, and I stood above him, just staring down.

Then I started laughing, laughing as hard as I ever had, and then he started half-moaning, half-laughing, and I could hear that old laugh of his, the one that starts deep in the pit of his stomach, that place a person falls into every day if he's really crazy, and then he sat up and laughed harder than me.

"Just needed that to straighten me out," he said. "I figured that one out the other night when Marlene was watching one of them old horror movies, you know, the lightning coming into a dark operating room straight into the monster's head."

I helped him up and brushed him off, noticing how he looked like he had just been brought back to life, like some cartoon character who had fallen off a cliff and hit bottom, only to get back up and miraculously resume the chase.

I wanted to hold him, maybe shake him up a bit out of relief, or anger, I didn't know which. But I didn't. Friends like we are don't do that kind of thing. A friend just goes with you on something, wherever you're going, or does whatever you're doing. No comment is needed to hold up their end.

And that's what it was all the way home, no comment about the cables. We stopped at the Hofbrau for a six to go and then cracked one open for each of us and drank it in the gravel lot of the bar, both of us staring up at the darkening sky, a few stars just beginning to show. I wanted to speak, but we stayed silent as we drank and then jumped back in and jammed up the radio.

On the way back home, I could still smell the odor of electricity in the cab. A smell I thought seemed like what burnt stars must smell like. Cofer was still laughing, drinking a last road beer. Before he dropped me off, we swung toward his house, and Cofer shut of his lights while we drifted past his picture window. Marlene was lifting the baby up into the air and then bringing her down gently against her knee. I could hear Cofer weakening, and when Marlene stood up and walked toward the Christmas tree holding his daughter's hand, I knew he'd cave in.

After he dropped me off in my driveway, I knew he'd go back home like he always does and sit up half the night in the living room. Marlene would be asleep on the couch, the baby tight under her arms, and Cofer would be cleaning his shotgun. His mind would be fluttering like a confusion of birds lifting off in a forest. He'd get the urge to just drive, leave in the middle of the night and drive until he collapsed. But he would stay home like he always did and stand over the baby's bed for ten or fifteen minutes, watching her chest lift up and down like there were delicate wings beating inside of her.

When I went to bed, all I could smell was that blue arc lifting him off the ground, and I fell asleep to the memory of the sound of his jumper cables dangling over the tailgate, bouncing and hitting the freshly plowed blacktop, then striking against the back of his truck, the rhythm of tiny sparks as they clicked together spitting into the night.

Perfect Bass

We were out in the lily pads on Bridge Lake. It was over-cast, but God, was it hot. Must have been ninety degrees. Willis was rowing, or at least trying to row. He isn't much good at rowing. He makes too much noise when he lets the end of the oar drop into the lake. My dad taught me years ago to let the oars go in real slow-like, and then when you lift them up to draw your backstroke, you push down on the end of the handle and lift the oars up in the air a little bit and the water slides down near your hands, and then you slip the oar back into the water and row silently. No noise from dripping. Nothing. Just stalking bass.

But Willis doesn't fish that way. He likes to make noise. Lots of noise. He claims it will attract fish. So he always brings along his ghetto blaster with plenty of cassettes of Creedence Clearwater Revival. He likes them best.

"A real rock-and-roll band," he says, "not one of them queer bands dressed up like women."

So the night we caught Murphy (that's what I call the bass now), Willis was blasting "Oh Lord, Stuck in Lodi," and I was sure every creature in the lake could feel the vibrations of John Fogerty ripping into every guitar lick. Willis took me deep into the pads, as deep as we'd ever been. He was huffing and puffing, trying to get the johnboat we use as far into the outlet as we could go. "Let it rip," he said, and I threw my lure as far as I could up into the shallows.

Me and Willis fish exclusively with "Da Rat," a kind of crude plastic mouse with a real soft body and hooks that disappear when it sits on top of the water. But when a fish hits it, the body just gives way and hooks bust into the fish's mouth and there you go . . . you got yourself a ride, as me and Willis say.

This night Willis was very specific in his advice; usually he goes for more generalities, like, "Just toss it over that way," or his favorite: "Fish have brains the size of peas. You ought to be able to catch one or two tonight." But tonight he stood up while he rowed, scouting, as he liked to say. He had on his Polaroids, and in the fading light he said he could see down through the six feet of water, right to the sand, "even under them pads," he was saying.

Suddenly he jerked backward and started hollering, "Holy shit, there's a monster! The monster of all monsters, right over there by that stump! Cast that Rat up there and let her sit." Willis pointed out the spot, and I let Da Rat go in a perfect arched trajectory. We both watched it lift off into the sky and then splat loudly right next to the stump. "Good," said Willis. "Now let the rings die . . . don't even move that mother until it's absolutely still as still."

We stood in the boat and waited. "Not yet," he'd say. "Let them all die. All the rings coming out from that lure hitting the water are like sending a telegram to that bass. Let the rings die, and then strip that Rat back slower than you care to . . . slow . . . real slow."

I did what he said. I couldn't bear it long. I hate retrieving slow. I like to rip the plugs over the surface of the water and then let them sit, and then twitch them like they were wounded, or better yet, crazed with fear, but not Willis. He sometimes took an hour to retrieve a bait fifty yards. He'd reel one crank and then let the bait sit on the water. Twitch it just a bit, the tiniest of rings rippling out in the still water, and then he'd repeat the same pattern, only with a slight variation. "You got to vary your twitches," he'd say. "Bass go for wounded bait fish . . . just like I'm makin' this lure look . . . see?" and he'd twitch the bait and make the lure turn on its side and wiggle a little. "Looks like a wounded frog, don't it?" he'd say.

A minute into the retrieve and wham-o, a truck hit the Rat. Willis was jumping and screaming, "Hot damn!" he was shouting. "Hot damn! You got that mother! Now take him easy . . . don't let him break you off in them weeds . . . he'll lose you if you do that . . . just hold tight on him," he whooped.

Ten minutes of shouting and jumping around in the boat, almost capsizing, and we had Murphy up to the net. Twenty-eight inches of largemouth gaping up at us. "Sweet mama," Willis said, "that looks like a record fish. What a hunk of bass!" he shouted, lifting the fish by his lower lip and bringing it up to my face. Behind us I could hear Creedence singing, "Got to set down, take a rest on the porch," and I thought about Willis and me stepping up to my own back porch with Willis's wife, Connie, and my wife, Ulene, drinking mai tais in the heat and me holding Murphy. "This is one big damn fish," Willis said, and we shook hands, and then we each tipped a Labatt's back and drank as fast as we could.

"Now what?" I said.

"Whadya mean now what?" Willis said. "We take him home and fry him up, have a big dinner—there's enough meat for the whole block on him."

"Wait a minute," I said, "wait just a damn minute. This is a prize fish. What about that action mount with Da Rat I've been talkin' about for over my workbench?"

"Naw," Willis said, "he's food . . . big food."

"Well how about if I call Fatty Corson and tell him we got this fish on one of the lures from his store? Maybe he'll give us some free stuff, and we'll get our picture thumbtacked up around his register. We'll be bass pros."

Then it hit me: We were holding about six pounds of live bass. Big Bass. The kind of bass hicks from Indiana catch on all those Sunday morning fishing shows. This bass is worth its weight in gold, I told Willis.

"We'll stuff him," I said.

"With cranberries and small potatoes, and then we'll eat him, right?"

"Nope," I said. "We take him home, put him in the aquarium, and really stuff him. I mean we'll feed Murphy here until he bulks up, and then we'll catch him again."

"You mean we'll force feed him and then bring him back out here, let him loose and then catch him again? Fat chance, you dumb ass. He'll just head for cover as soon as he gets back in there. And besides, it's slightly illegal to harbor game fish. Remember a few years ago when they nabbed Heinzelman for keeping that trout in his kid's aquarium?"

"Oh no he won't. We'll dump the beer in the boat and fill up the cooler, keep some of the ice, and we'll keep him alive until we get home. And since when did you worry about anything being illegal, Mr. Across-the-border-fire-works Dealer?"

"But why do you want to make him bigger? He might

not taste as good. You know if they get too big, they get too tough."

"We'll get him up to about twelve pounds, and then we'll invent a lure and say we caught him on it ... and you know what that means? A million bucks, easy. Look at all those guys like Babe Winkelman and Bobby Joe Wonders, those guys that catch all those bass in the south. They always endorse lures. Like that "Big Mamma" we bought last year—looked like a clothes pin with a French Tickler tied to it."

"Yeah, and it didn't catch nothin'," Willis said, "except a catfish. A surface lure that caught a damn catfish."

"Well, see what I mean?" I said. "We get us a twelve-pound largemouth and design some kind of goofy lure, and we got ourselves a TV show. We got ourselves a million bucks selling the rights to our lure, and then we got us a house in Florida."

So we dumped the beer, added some ice and weeds to the lukewarm pond water in the cooler and rowed Murphy across the pond. All the way home Willis sat in the back making sure Murphy was still alive. He'd holler up a report every once in a while, "Murphy's finning fine," and then he'd laugh and whoop and turn the blaster up higher. Mostly Murphy seemed to tolerate the ride. By the time we got to my house he seemed a bit shell-shocked. Maybe from Willis's constant fondling, I don't know. When we ran inside, the girls were shouting in their drunken voices, "Hey boys, what you got there, a couple of crappies?" and they laughed and held their stomachs. They were almost naked, sporting new underwear, bought, they hooted, to "get our minds off of fish for a change." They pranced around the hallway, giggling and pretending to walk like models, and it was Eulene who started to take off her bra first, and for the first time in my life I told her to go to bed without me. I knew what had to be done, and Eulene and Connie would never let up once they got us going. So we lifted Murphy out of the water and chased them out into the backyard where they fell into the tent we have up for the entire summer and passed out immediately.

That night Willis and I sat in the bathroom listening to old '60s rock and roll, drinking beer, and occasionally slapping high fives across the wet tiles. When I woke up, Willis was asleep with his head on the toilet, and my hand was still in the tub. I could feel Murphy swish by and then watched him circle around the weeds we'd thrown in for him, a few lily pads floating up near the faucets. I turned the lights down and just watched him hunkered down under one of the pads. His jaw moved slowly and his gills opened and closed as if he were about to die of relaxation. He showed no sign of being afraid, just relaxed and holding there six inches above the plastic flamingoes glued to the bottom of the tub to keep you from slipping in the shower. He was beautiful . . . a million-dollar fish living in a sixty-dollar bathtub.

I bought a big air pump to keep Murphy full of oxygen, and I kept him in the tub until January, when I moved him into an old Amana I used to smoke fish in but gutted out and moved into the back room. Then I started experimenting.

Willis would come over almost very night and help me make up the tiny cotton balls. We'd soak them in the flavors we thought Murphy would go for and then drop them over the side of the fridge. One by one we'd let them fall: chicken soup, tomato soup, vanilla; we even tried stuff like Cheese Whiz and balls of Spam we rolled in our fingers, but he never touched one of them.

All in all, we dropped over a hundred flavors right on his head and they just sank to the bottom. All he wanted was worms. Crawlers . . . the bigger the better. I'd slip into Buck's Bait every week and buy three or four dozen, and every time, Buck himself would step out from behind the one-way glass in his office and stand behind Rudy, the clerk. "You must be eating these goddamn things, Ed. That's about twenty dozen in the last two months." And each time I'd say, "You bet your ass, Buck . . . love em' fried, sautéed, use 'em in my eggs every day," and I'd walk out.

In mid-February I was working on the light over Murphy's "pond," oiling up a locked up pivot nut with some WD-40 when I dropped a Q-tip by accident and Murphy hit it almost as soon as it hit the water. I thought he'd choke on it but he turned and swam straight for the bottom, then just sulked in the seaweed I'd planted. I watched him for over two hours, hoping he wouldn't just croak and float belly-up, but he just stayed there, finning slowly and staring at the underwater mural I'd made out of plastic table mats from Money's restaurant I'd fastened to the inside of the tank.

Thinking it must have been the shape, I tied up a silver marabou streamer and wiggled it through the water with some ten-pound mono. Nothing.

Murphy just stayed exactly where he was. Then I noticed the rainbow of oil on the surface of the water . . . WD-40. I tied up another marabou and sprayed the hell out of it and then let it slip into the water. Murphy shot out from under the weeds, and it was all I could do to keep it out of his mouth.

That night we tried twenty pellets soaked in WD-40, and Murphy ate every one, slashing and charging like a small shark.

"We need a lure soaked in this stuff," Willis said, smiling.

"All we need, Willis, is anything soaked in this stuff. Murphy would eat a turd if I sprayed it with this," I said. "Now all we have to do is concoct some goofy looking lure, like my minnow here, soak it in this WD, and then take Murphy into Buck's and register the catch. We'll get a picture of you and me with the lure and Murphy—a sure thing. Those guys at Berkley Lures will be calling us the next day, I bet. A world record bass on Ed's Minnow."

"What about my name?" Willis asked.

"We'll tell them in the directions to give it the Willis dying minnow twist, how's that? Besides, I caught the damn fish."

"Yeah well, I got guide's rights. I led you right to him. I know you made a good cast an' all, but I took us in."

"Okay, okay . . . a fifty-fifty split on profits, but my name's on the box."

"Deal," Willis said. And from now on I'm the technician here. I do the soaking in the WD-40, and you make the minnows, partner."

The rest of the month we fed Murphy like he was a prize Hereford. We soaked french fries in the WD, and Murphy ballooned up almost in front of our eyes. In early March we both figured he was around twelve pounds, healthy as hell and full of piss and bad temper. He was a bass to be reckoned with, Willis said the night all hell broke loose.

We were up late, drinking beer as usual, feeding Murphy, when I heard Ulene holler from the front room about a blue car with a light on top pulling up to the house. I thought it might be another one of her stunts, like that time she told me that the Prize Patrol was at the door, and I came flying through the living room, only to stop dead in my tracks, because she had covered herself with sequins and wanted me to watch her new belly dancing routine. But this time, when I looked through the blinds, I saw the car.

"Holy shit," Willis said, "it's Lutz. Jesus, we'll both go to jail. What'll we do Ed?"

"You stall him—I'll take Murphy."

"Take him? Take him where? Christ, he'll suffocate, Ed," Willis said.

"I got all that worked out, Willis," I said. "Been thinking about this happening all along. You know how secrets don't stay secrets too long. Well, I been waiting for Lutz to stick his fat ass in here. Just keep him at the door until I get out of here."

Willis headed for the living room, and I could hear Lutz hollering through the door, "This is the DNR. I'm coming in one way or the other. I have reason to believe you're harboring a game fish in this house."

Before I heard him break the door down, I was out the back and into the car. Murphy was right beside me in an old Coleman cooler. I closed the lid and turned on the pump—a little six-volt job I'd found at the hardware store in the tropical fish section.

I hit the tape deck, and me and Murphy headed for Bud's pond. I sang all the way out there, stopping every mile or two to check him. He looked good in there; maybe he sensed he was going home. "Put me in coach, I'm ready to play," I sang and ran my hands down his side . . . twenty pounds of largemouth bass at my fingertips. He'd grown used to me, like a pet, and I could reach down and touch him anytime I wanted. I dropped in a big crawler soaked in oil and shut the lid.

It was cold at the pond . . . an early March night with a big wind . . . maybe twenty degrees windchill. I hauled the cooler out of the car. Doused the headlights and felt my way over the ice, thin now, and clear of snow. Black ice you could see through on a sunny day. The ice up here in early March is tricky: sometimes there's a patch or two of even thinner ice where springs come in to feed the pond. I inched my way toward the center, the spud hanging on a cord bouncing on the ice.

I checked Murphy one last time and started the hole. I could hear Lutz's siren coming through town, and by the time I was through, I could see his headlights through the woods. I picked Murphy up and took out a tiny flashlight I had taken from Ulene's purse and wrapped with water-proof tape. I tied the light to Murphy's tail and let him slip through the ice. I knew it would probably go out in a matter of seconds, but I figured it would stay on long enough to let me know he'd headed for the bottom.

I let Murphy slide through the hole and then lay down with my hands over my eyes, staring into absolute black-ness. Below me the flashlight looked like a faint, lone eye staring at the sky, getting smaller and smaller. Then I lost sight of it. Murphy was on the bottom, I hoped, hunkered down for the rest of the winter and like me, waiting for spring.

When I stood up, Lutz caught me in the eyes with his flashlight, one of those big long black jobs with a hundred batteries in it.

"All right, you son of a bitch," he said. "Where's the fish?

"Fish?" I said. "Haven't caught any."

"You lying bastard, Eddie. I know you got a fish—a big bass. It's all over town. Now where the hell is he?"

"I got nothing Lutz," I said. "I'm fishing here . . . smelt. See," I said, holding up the tiny ultra-light rod I'd managed to stuff into the pocket of my snowmobile suit on the way out the door.

He was right in my face, and I could feel the heat from the bulb against my cheek.

"You're lucky. I know you had him," Lutz said, turning around. "Just watch your ass. I'm always around, you know. They'll be a next time, too, Eddie. I'll write you up before you can find the time to spit."

I watched him head back to his cruiser, and then I saw Willis pull in beside him. Lutz drove off, back to town, I suppose, maybe stopping at the Log Cabin Cafe for a coffee or a game of pool. All I know is that me and Willis just lay there on the ice in our snowmobile suits until daylight, drinking beer and freezing our asses off. We'd cup our hands and look down through the clear ice into the dark water. Once or twice we spotted the light on Murphy's tail, and then it must have gone out, but we didn't care. We felt good, even though we knew Murphy was swimming free fifty feet below us. We both knew we'd be back in June, opening day of bass season . . . armed with Ed's Minnow and enough WD-40 to float a battleship.

Mystery Park

Ray Munger was holed up in the Mercury Motel just east of Negaunee, looking out the window to check the Ryder rental truck parked outside his room. Experience had taught him that even in the U.P., teenage vandals would think nothing of trashing the cab for the standard CB radio or the chrome mirrors he had insisted be installed so he could negotiate "idiot traffic" in the city. He'd driven in after a late start from Wausau, crossing into the U.P. just about dark. The next morning he'd be up early, headed for Munising to help move his sister to the lower peninsula, piano and all, where she had decided to cohabitate with her illiterate boyfriend in Grand Rapids.

He watched the last moths of the summer spiraling in the early October air in the vapor light hanging over the parking lot. Then he looked at the new tattoo on his right biceps. The day before, coming off a three-day drunk, he had walked into the only tattoo parlor in Wausau and ordered up a picture of Elvis Presley. Now he stared directly into the King's vacant, ink-stained eyes. The tattoo artist had gotten the hair almost perfect, but the Elvis sneer looked more like the face you might see on a cartoon character, say, Elmer Fudd, rather than the sneer that made young girls shed their panties on countless trips into the cloisters of Graceland. Plus, the tattoo looked too large for the space the artist had put him in. Elvis looked cramped and tired, his face spilling over into the confines of Ray's lower shoulder and part of his armpit.

Outside, on the front lawn of the motel, Ray could see the light glinting off the aluminum replica of the first Mercury Spacecraft, a symbol not only for the motel, but also a "genuine tourist attraction for the town, a real money mill," the manager had told him when he signed in. The mock-up was stuck on the end of a steel pole directly in front of the motel, and from a distance it looked more like a giant trashcan or a flask than a space capsule. Just before he'd walked into his room, Ray had climbed the observation ladder and looked inside. The owners had positioned a mannequin at the controls with an old

Time Magazine cover of Alan Shepard's face pasted over it.

"Looks just like him don't it?" the manager had said over his shoulder. But all Ray thought about was how much it looked like something you'd see in K-Mart or Giantway, the way its hands were tied around an old car steering wheel, the helmet made out of a five gallon dry-wall bucket painted silver, with vacuum cleaner hoses leading to a space suit that looked more like two inflat-able air mattresses tied together, which is exactly what it was. "Looks just like old Alan, teeth and all," Ray said, climbing back down the ladder and walking toward his room.

Ray really had three things on his mind at once: His botched sneer tattoo; the waitress he had brushed up against more than once at the Dumpling House, where he'd eaten three helpings of strudel dumplings before he hit the motel; and the caged bear he'd seen at Sonny Bob's Mystery Park on the outskirts of Ishpeming. Initially, he intended to drive right past the spot because he had seen signs for miles saying, "Sonny Bob's Mystery Park, Tour-ists Welcome," and he didn't want to feel like any sort of tourist.

But he slowed down when he saw the bear cage snugged up against the gas station, originally an Old Tex-aco stop, now painted over with Shell signs, the red ves-tiges of the Texaco flying horse jutting up from behind the edge of the giant shell on the sign. "You can trust your

car to the man who wears the star, the Red Texaco Star,"
Ray sang to himself, remembering the Sullivan show and
the countless times he had seen Russian Bear acts and
then the commercials, thinking how pathetic the bears
looked in tutus carrying umbrellas or spinning plates on
the ends of sticks.

When he pulled in, there were six or seven men in
flannel shirts standing around the cage. Bear hunters, he
learned, all of them anxious to get close enough to touch
what was once a wild Northern Michigan black bear now
reduced to pacing a small cage while a television flashed
inside the store, its sound piped into the cage via an old
public address speaker wired to the top of the cage. The
sign over the cage read: "*Ursus Americanus* American
Black Bear, but you can call him Ollie."

Between swigs of beer, Sonny told Ray it was his brilliant idea five years before to take in the orphaned cub
and teach him tricks so that he could dance and spin umbrellas in the cage to attract tourists into his Mystery Park,
where he had built a series of optical illusions to make
people think the land the park occupied was haunted by
"Indian spirits." In one corner of the Mystery House you
could sit in a chair and the room seemed to tip forty-five
degrees away from you, the sun miraculously turning
ninety degrees to make it appear to be traveling horizon-
tally rather than vertically.

In another room a medicine ball painted with Indian
designs would roll uphill, and in the "Ojibway Burial

Chamber" Sonny had arranged a skeleton with arrows stuck in the cavity where the heart would have been with a sign that read, "On this site Chief Dancing Eagle was found without his heart. Some say that if you put your ear to the ground and listen, you will still hear it beating." Sure enough, if you bent down, you could hear the faint lub-dub, lub-dub of a human heart beating underground, which was really a cassette tape loop fed into a galvanized trash can Sonny had buried five feet under the floor of the room. By the end of the story, Sonny was a bit thick in the tongue and listing to one side. He announced that he was going to bed "asap."

Ray Munger watched the bear pace back and forth and became even more aware of the ruined tattoo on his arm. In a fit he had pulled in at a rest stop, taken the bandage off, and tried to alter the face with an ink pen, but had made it look worse. He had rewrapped it with a Red Wings T-shirt and had driven on, the lettering on the Wings emblem blazing as red as blood on top of his arm. He was just about to unwrap it again, when three of the hunters approached the cage, taking up places opposite each other. They took turns thrusting their lit cigarettes into the bear, driving him back against the other side of the cage where another hunter would do the same thing, the bear careening in a frenzy from side to side.

"Let up on him!" Ray shouted.

"What's it to you, anyway?" one of the hunters shouted back.

"If he was loose, you wouldn't be doing that. He'd have one of your fat heads snapped off in a second," Ray said.

"Well, he ain't loose, so I guess we'll never know, dickhead," one of the older ones said, moving toward him.

"I been in a cage, just about that size," Ray lied. "Just got out of Jackson Prison two weeks ago, and I don't feel so good. So don't screw with me. I got heat," Ray said, patting under his left arm.

The men parted and trailed off. One moved close enough to smell Ray's dumpling breath, and Ray patted under his arm again to warn him off. Ray moved toward the front of the cage and watched the bear turn in smaller and smaller circles, then finally sit down in a heap in the center of the cage.

"Exhausted," he said. "Not much of a life for a bear, is it?" he said into the cage.

Sonny ran out from the station.

"What in the hell is going on?"

"Your bear here looks a little frazzled."

"Yeah, well, sometimes that happens. I just cover him up for the night and tomorrow morning he'll be good as new," Sonny said, drawing a blue tarp around the cage, with the words "Do Not Touch The Bear Cage," mislettered so that it read more like *donut* than *do not.*

"Aren't you worried someone will steal him? Or at least let him out?" Ray asked.

"Ollie's been out here for five years, when the weather's good. In the winter I keep him in the cooler out back.

No one is dumb enough to let him out. He'd probably bite your hand off in the trying. Besides, he likes it here. I doubt he'd leave."

Ray watched Sonny go back into the station and turn on the single light over the cash register. He watched him pocket the cash from the till; then he closed the door and set the deadbolt but left the television blaring behind the window.

"He likes Letterman!" he shouted through the window and then disappeared.

Ray slipped his hands between the edges of the tarp and watched Ollie staring up at the screen. He made a sound like a whisper and the bear turned his head. He could see the bear's dark eyes, wet and shining in the half light from the screen.

"I'll be back later, buckaroo," he whispered and then drove to his room at the Mercury Motel and took a shower.

At eleven-thirty the diner lights went out, and the waitress he'd been watching locked up and headed down Main Street. Ray caught up with her. She was tall and long-legged and had long hair that looked like the wind was inside of it—wild and almost careless.

"Hey," he said.

"Hay is for horses," she said and kept walking. "Want a beer?" Ray said.

"With you?"

"Well, with us," Ray said. "Me and Elvis." He turned his

arm toward her under the streetlight.

"If that's Elvis, I'm Meryl Streep," she said.

"Well, look at the hair, a perfect wave, and if you could turn his head around he'd have a perfect DA. The face needs a little work; I got to go back through Negaunee on my way home, and I'll get it fixed there. But for now, let's get a beer."

"My husband doesn't like me to get late-night beers," she said.

"Well, how about just this one night you tell him you went bowling with Elvis," Ray said, dipping toward her chest and stopping short at her name tag, "Miss Marie?"

"All right, all right, one beer. I don't know what I'm doing this for. But let's go," she laughed. "Just make sure Elvis there keeps his lips tucked up under your shirt."

They walked down the street and stopped in front of the fake capsule outside the motel.

"I'm staying here," Ray said.

"Up there?" she asked, pointing to the nose cone.

"Jeesh, no," Ray said. "In a room. I always park in the back. I got a big Ryder truck. On my way to help my sister move to Grand Rapids. I got a winch in the back of that truck," he said.

"You moving an elephant or something?" she laughed.

"No, just a piano, a big upright that's worth more to me as firewood. So I thought I'd tie it off and winch her up into the truck and then winch her out down there in Grand Rapids, or maybe when we're rolling about sixty

I'll set it up so the winch just kind of lets the piano out the back, and goodbye, I won't have to unload the damned thing."

She motioned toward the bar, really the lounge in the Timberlanes Bowling Alley, where they were bowling with special night lights.

"Just our luck," she said. "Starlight bowling." Inside, there were black lights over every alley, and the balls were marked with fluorescent tape so they reflected light on their way down the lanes. Each pin had tape around the top, and when someone got a strike all you could see were flashes of light shooting out into the bar.

They sat in a corner and ordered beers, and then more beers, the sound of pins exploding mingling in their conversation, the strobe lights glinting off their eyes as they moved closer to each other.

"I don't have a husband," she finally said.

"I figured as much," he said. "I don't have a wife. I got a sister, and I got a ragged-ass tattoo, but I don't have a wife."

Ray was watching the pin-setter sweep over the fallen pins, then rise up, get a new rack, and set them back down.

"I want to go get that bear," he said out of the blue.

"What?" she said.

"I want to head for Sonny's Mystery Park, get that bear, and let him go."

"You can't do that—set a bear loose around here."

"Why not? There's bears all over here."

"Well, you got me there," Marie said. "But don't you think it's a little dangerous to just open his cage? You'd have to run pretty fast if he decides to shoot the gap."

"The winch will take care of that. We'll pull up, hook the cage on the winch and pull it up the ramp, and then, we're gone. We take him a few miles up north and let him go."

"I'm in," she said. "I hate seeing him in there every night watching that stupid television. All he does is pace and sit all day. Sonny don't care much for him either, throws some food in there once in a while. Most of what he gets, he gets from the tourists. Sonny sells peanuts and popcorn to feed him at a buck a bag."

"Let's go," Ray said, pulling on her arm. They walked back down Main Street and into the motel parking lot. Marie stood under the capsule and looked up.

"I remember him going up in that thing. The first man from the United States to ride a rocket."

"Yeah, and I heard he had to pee, so they shut down the electricity in his space suit, and then he let it go, just like that, peed right in his spacesuit. Then they started her up again, and he just took off into the sky."

"Let's take another look at him up there," she said. "Maybe we can get in this time."

They climbed the steps to the hatch and looked in. Shepard was still in there, his grin illuminated by a bank of tiny green Christmas lights blinking on and off. "Let's get in," she said, "just for a minute."

"Okay, but be careful, there's not much room," he said. "Be careful, lots of sharp edges."

"Jeez, it's tight in here," she said. "I don't like this much."

"Come on, now," Ray said. "You wanted to come up here." He reached for her shirt.

"Not now, Ray, I don't even know you. We got bear work to do. Just kiss me up here. I want to feel what it's like to kiss in space," she said.

He leaned toward her, and then she wrapped her arms around him.

"Ouch!" he shouted. "Watch Elvis. He's still wet."

"Well, let's go," she said. "We'll come back after we pick up Ollie and let him loose."

Ray cruised into Sonny's Mystery Park with no lights, stopping fifty feet from the cage. He leaned out the window and took one shot with his Crossman pellet rifle—the one he'd remembered to throw under the seat for protection in Grand Rapids—knocking out the vapor light over the cage.

"What if Sonny hears us?" Marie said.

"His house is a mile back down the road," Ray said. "By the time he gets out here, we'll be long gone."

He backed in, got out, and opened the truck door, extended the ramp, and then pulled the cable out from the winch. Ollie was sitting perfectly still, watching the test pattern on the television. Ray hooked up the cage and hit the winch button, sliding Ollie up the ramp and into the truck.

"See," he said. "Easy, easy. Who said it's hard to steal a bear?"

They headed north out of town, passing a few cars. She sat next to him, running her hand up his leg as he drove.

"Later," he said. "We got a bear to let loose." She fiddled with the radio, settling on Waylon Jennings.

"I love Waylon," she said, putting her head on his shoulder.

"Not as good as Elvis," Ray said. "But close."

"Very close," she said, leaning over to kiss his neck. "You let me at that tattoo tonight, and I'll straighten out that mouth of his," she laughed.

Ray slowed the truck and wheeled down a two-track, then stopped in a clearing and doused the lights.

They got out and stood looking up at the sky.

"This is where you really see the stars," she said. "I know almost all the constellations. When I was a kid I had one of those plastic planetariums you could project onto your bedroom ceiling. I learned them all. There's Cassiopeia and Orion. And my favorite, the Big Dipper."

Ray just looked into the sky.

"All I know is the Big Dipper, Ursa Major," he said. "And the northern lights. And everything else I know is that we got a bear in a rental truck, and if the police find us we're in shit deep enough to drown. Stealing bears I would guess is worth about ninety days and a lot of cash."

He hooked the cage up to a tree with rope, jumped back in the truck and then pulled ahead. The crate slid down the ramp.

"What now?" she said.

"Easy," he said. "We open the cage. You get in the truck and I'll pop the door."

She jumped into the cab, and Ray reached for the latch on the cage. In the light from his lantern he could see Ollie's eyes. They looked fiercer now, he thought. Wild. They looked like eyes that wanted to go somewhere, he kept thinking. He popped the dead bolt, and the door swung open, and then he ran to the cab and jumped in. He leaned out the window and put the light on Ollie as he walked out into the night.

"I thought he'd roar or something," she said.

"Me too," Ray said. "Except Sonny had him so brain-washed, he'll probably head for the first house where he can watch television through the front window," he laughed.

Instead, Ollie sat down at the edge of the two-track. "If he stays there all night, he'll never get into the swamp. Do something," she said.

Ray reached for the pellet gun and aimed for his lower back.

"Right in the ass," he said as Ollie shot up from the

ground and ran toward the woods. "A minute ago, I thought about killing him right there where he sat," Ray said.

"Killing him?" she said. "Why would you want to do that?"

"Because he ain't wild anymore, but then I figured, so what. At least give him the chance to be wild again. It's better than nothing."

"Nice," she said. "Very nice, Ray. You did a nice thing for that bear, and I hope he's happy out there in the swamp."

"Staring up at the stars," Ray said.

All the way back to town, Ray was thinking of the way her leg felt against his. He alternated between thinking about Ollie sniffing swamp air for the first time in years—how it must have felt to him to have the wild freedom to move without bumping into something—and thinking about Marie. And he wondered about getting back up into the capsule with her, how it would feel to sit up there until daybreak, looking up through the hatch cover, really an old washing machine cover from the Laundromat. They could count stars, he thought; they could rearrange Elvis' face. For the first time in years Ray would know what it meant to feel how his skin fit his body exactly, how right everything would feel with her, and then he would think of Ollie moving though swamp and tangle, his body perfect in all the space that surrounded him.

As If We Were Prey

Thirty years of teaching, George Houck was thinking, was like hacking through lunch meat, a phrase he'd remembered from the only novel he'd ever read. He was sitting in his office overlooking the student parking lot, recovering from his first-hour independent shop class—"felon-ed," he called it. Behind him, out in the shop, "the rejects," as he called them, in his fourth-hour class were sweeping up as the end of the hour approached. Even with his back to them, he could name exactly the time when Jimmy Fitzgerald would hit the switch to turn on the dust suction system, and Derald Metzger would say,

"Suck it up Jimmy, suck the big one," and Jimmy would say, in his clipped, harelipped voice, "I'm sucking, I'm sucking," and then he'd hit the switch and contort his mouth into a perfect circle, pretending to suck all the air and whatever else he could imagine into his mouth.

The rest of the boys would be lining the sink, laughing and flipping water at each other, slamming the curved water bar with their feet. And Houck knew the exact time he'd hear the paper towel dispenser start in, the boys wringing sheet after sheet of cheap brown drying towels into each other's hands. Fitzgerald would be sweeping the shop well past the time the door clicked shut, and Houck would have to go out and remind him to eat lunch. "Jimmy," he'd say, "get your goofy ass to lunch," and Jimmy would waddle off, grinning.

Today, like all his other days, he didn't need to watch to see what they were up to. Instead, he went through a checklist of what was left of his capacity. In thirty years he had seen it all. He had seen kids OD in the early '70s and still carried the specter of Jimmy Brozo writhing to death in front of the principal's office, a victim of taking too many dog tranquilizers. He had seen kids fucking inside their lockers, and once, in the early '80s, he had watched Jerald Christensen stiff-leg up the front walk, a shotgun concealed in his pants, shouting for Lyle Harwood, the principal, to get his ass out of his office to face some justice. He had seen hour after hour of cruel jokes, jeering, and taunting, and he remembered watching Dick

Louchart in the faculty parking lot try to fend off his own entire machine-shop class, battling back from the roof of his Jeep, brandishing a tire iron.

This semester was no different from the last one, and Houck was famous for saying, "The names change but not the faces, never the fucking faces," or his other personal favorite, "You can't polish a horse turd." Jimmy Fitzgerald had taken shop all four years of school, and to Houck, he was like some kind of lost son. But today, payday, Houck was doing his math, like he always did, checking "the suits, the accounting boys, the pinheads" as he called them. He heard the vacuum system go on, heard the laughter, the water bar clumping. That was his cue, the water bar on the half-circle sink. They expected him to walk out of his office, lean against the doorway and say, "Get out of here, you pussies." But today, he just sat. There was silence for almost a minute, and then he heard the sound of farm boys heading out to lunch. He didn't feel much like calling them pussies today, he thought, even though they were. Thirty years was taking its toll, his face setting up like so much plaster.

Houck knew the pallor that came over older teachers, the way their skin grew paler and paler by the day. He blamed most of it on fluorescent light mixed with the tiny particles of chalk dust that were always in the air. He had a theory about florescent light and chalk dust: he called it "that teacher make-up," a chemical reaction between skin and dust, the light that shot out of a tube and the dead-end target of a face in the same room for too many days in a row. Bombarded, he thought, as though he were in a particle accelerator, his head locked in a high-tech vise, thirty years of juvenile venom piercing his skin at the speed of light.

Back in his chair he was doing a new kind of math, multiplying his thirty years times 180, computing the number of days he'd worked. Minus a few sick days, twelve to be exact, in thirty years, he came up with 5,388. He felt his skin crawl back against his scalp and thought of himself walking into Grayling High School thirty years before, in '66. Crew-cut clean, he came straight from Da Nang into the classroom, said he still had "gook shit stuck in his 'Nam boots." Back then he wasn't afraid to cuff one of the boys once in a while, or shout over the joiners and saws. That's when he started his pussies line, only back then he'd said "you goddamn pussies." The next day after he said it was the first time he was in Jim Stripes's office, humbled enough to promise to talk to every kid's parents and send a letter of apology to each one.

Now, thinking of that first day, he was wondering how just one day had stretched into 5,388. He was thinking about all the nine-week projects he'd graded, how many routered signs he'd read with goofy spellings or slogans that ran off the end of the wood. At one time he'd counted 238 signs that read, "Why are there so many more horses asses than horses?" a total surpassed only by his count of 302 "No Trespassing" signs spelled incorrectly. He

laughed to himself when he remembered Del Corey mis-
spelling *trespassing*, substituting an *i* for the *a*, the whole
school teasing him about not allowing anyone to piss on
his dad's lawn. He thought of how many lamps he'd seen
made, or how many times he'd told kids not to cut when
they weren't looking, and sure enough, he'd be holding
somebody's finger in his hand, and shaking it at the rest
of the class. "Just be glad," he'd say, "just be glad this ain't
something else you cut off," holding it high over the
heads of farm boys looking up into the fierce lights hanging like long thin clouds over the woodshop.

He'd seen Darrel Metzger almost bleed to death from
a deep ripsaw cut across his left forearm, and now he
looked toward a faded newspaper clipping on his bul-
letin board of what he was years ago, standing next to
Derald Sr. (nicknamed Derailed), Metzger's dad, at the
Michigan High School shop exposition in East Lansing,
both of them admiring Herb's rolltop desk, the blue ribbon, "Best of Show" dangling from one drawer-pull like
some kind of appendage.

Houck stood up, thinking back through all these mo-
ments, thinking of the bombardment his face had taken
in thirty years, and something snapped. Maybe it was the
sound the broom made when Jimmy Fitzgerald hit the
base of the planer like he did every day, a sharp whack
that echoed off the far wall and came back through him
like a line drive, or maybe it was just the sharp smell of
October, a month he cordoned off on his calendar each

year, the first weekend ablaze with dark red marker and the word DUCKS blasted across Friday, Saturday, and Sunday: "Opening Weekend of Duck Season," it said, bordered with tiny exclamation points around the edges of those three days.

Snapped was what he thought when something shifted inside him and propelled him toward the door. By God, he was going a few days early, he thought. "Get your goofy ass to lunch," he said to Jimmy over his shoulder. Sick days, he thought, I'll take a couple of sick days, or business days. "Duck business days," he told the principal on his way out of the main office.

George Houck is buckled into in his Jeep Wagoneer, the one with camo seat covers and a duck's-head dash compass that waddles and turns when he changes direction, its bill moving when it hits true north. He is driving south to Pointe Mouillee near Saint Clair Shores to hunt ducks. He is a man who has already consumed a six pack of road beers, the last one dribbling down his crotch as he reached for the tape deck just outside Houghton Lake, the Doors at full blast, Houck singing "Break on Through to the Other Side" in the mid-Michigan twilight.

Houck is that rare kind of Western man who thinks of his life topographically. He sees in three dimensions, a Montagnard trick he learned in the Vietnam foothills from tribesmen who, legend said, could kill silently with their bare hands or telepathically, and who taught him that landscape could literally be taken inside. "You must learn to watch yourself moving through the jungle," he remembers the elders whispering to him. "Take the enemy inside with you, and when you come out, you will be alone, and your enemy will be no more."

Somewhere inside, Houck does, in fact, see himself moving. He sees the green hand of Michigan, the roll and curve as the roads wind farther north. Only he is driving due south into flat country, away from the hollow sinkhole he sees in the middle of his chest. Inside the darker, tangled regions of himself, he watches a shadow winding through jungle toward even darker places; places so low on a topo map they are marked below zero.

He is a man haunted by night sweats, dreams that come at him as if they were on television. He feels sometimes like he is standing still and that the world is flaring past him as if he were trapped in a shrapnel storm, everything sizzling past his face, cutting past his head. He is a man who has abandoned his job for a few days. Thirty years, minus twelve sick days, have accumulated in him like fallout. Like rain in a barrel. He needs, he knows, to get into the marsh, sip some hot coffee laced with Jack Daniels. He needs to forget Jimmy Fitzgerald, forget the sound of boys making things. He needs to forget the dust, the chalk, the lights. He needs to forget the dead-end life he has forged for himself. The divorce. The daughter who never writes. He needs to forget the fierce jungle fighter he once was, now turned into a flabby, pallid man. "A fucking lapdog squeezed out of the ass-end of a pit bull," he would tell you.

He imagines he is carrying the large bag of his life in the cargo area of the Jeep. What if he were to pull over at some darkened rest stop outside Detroit, pull the bag under a street lamp, and open it up? Reaching in there, he thinks, would be like reaching into a bag of snakes, each one full of a different kind of venom, each particular snake a manifestation of something he'd fucked up or guessed wrong on: like the decision to marry his first wife, both of them drunk and soaring on acid in Hawaii, taking her down under the pier and betting her she couldn't make him forget the noise of choppers in his head, the smell of jungle and blood he was sure was oozing from every pore, his skin turning to feathers when he thought he could fly.

Or the time he had forbidden his daughter to date Gil Godfrey, and she had snuck out, and they'd gotten in a wreck, her face a mass of shards. He knew the bag well, knew that every argument he'd ever had with his wife was in there, knew the loss of a stillborn son was tucked in one of its corners, knew that what little joy was left in his life was like dirt at the bottom.

If he could, he would cut out his own heart and hold it there in the driver's seat and examine it like someone else might examine a stone. He drives, purely from memory, south through Detroit and then east into flat, low country. He drives almost all afternoon, until he comes to the edge of a great swamp.

He stops at Billy's Bait and Bar, asks for a six of Moose-head to go, and then heads into marsh country: a thin wandering two-track covered by water most of the way. He's headed in, and he's watching himself like a god might be watching him, from above. A god who knows the darker regions of the lost places in his heart: the trail like a ribbon on a map, miles and miles of water, the blind only a tiny square stretched out below him in his imagi-nation. He's undergone a transformation. If you saw him now, you'd never put him back into Grayling. You would never imagine that he could stand next to a dunce like Derald Metzger and whisper for him to "cut the line." You'd never imagine that he could put up with the mo-notony of thirty years or let himself be bombarded by that kind of piercing light for so long. You'd imagine him like he was in the picture taken at Khe San, the sky gray and ugly, choppers coming in, Houck with his M16 in one hand, the other holding a fistful of black VC headbands like they were scalps.

At his parking area in the swamp, Houck's spot now for thirty years, he remembers he's early. *A day early, and illegal,* he laughs to himself, shouldering his twelve-gauge. *A fucking day early, and I'm here when I should be up there.* He slaps his knee, drops a box of magnums into his parka, and stomps off.

The path into the blind is really a long, winding sec-tion of plank walk, held up on stilts. He moves and weaves through the tall marsh grass, sometimes splitting it with his hands, other times merely parting it with his huge body. All the time, he's following himself, knows exactly where to turn before it comes up, sees the tiny dot of his body as if he were watching a radar screen, the "blip . . . blip . . . blip" sounding every time he's caught in the electron beam of the scanner. He stops frequently to catch his breath and to take in what he considers to be pure air: water and swamp air mixed with the slightly acrid odor of decay.

The blind is old, a squat stilt house covered with a collection of marsh grass and camo-net. There's a canoe to retrieve your kill, and inside, there are magazines scattered around a small table and an easy chair. The chair was his idea—an old La-Z-Boy from the '60s with beer holders duct taped to the arms. The magazine collection consists mostly of porno stuff, dropped off over the years by his other hunting buddies, guys who chipped in for the land and the blind and now come back only once every few years, some not at all. For all practical purposes, the blind is his.

Near dusk he sits back in the chair and opens the shooting window to the sky. He's drunk by now—drunk on beer and whiskey—and he's holding the gun like another man would cradle a woman's head. Sift through him now, and you'd find him lost, all notions of topography awash in alcohol, sorrow, the swill and spittle of thirty years of humping it through his life.

He fans the gun around the room, half-noticing the

way the light from the darkening sky catches in the tiny pores of his hands. From far off he hears the sound of ducks coming in. He knows, instinctively, that he can load six shells and fire six shots all within seconds and then load six more and six more. He could fire all fucking night, he shouts out loud to himself.

At the window he sees a flock of mallards coming in low to set down for the night. A day from now, he thinks, opening day, I'll have birds like that for lunch. But something rises in him that he recognizes but cannot place. He leans into the wind, into the last visible light of the day, and opens fire. Six shells and he's loading six more before the full flock can lift itself enough to escape. He's shooting, directly into the belly of the flock as it wheels past his head, shooting now through the roof, blowing holes in the thatched ceiling of the blind, his eyes covered with dust and smoke, the beer and whiskey drifting up toward the front of his mouth. In the seconds it takes all of this to happen, he sees himself in the back of his mind, standing in the bright light of a woodshop two hundred miles away, while all around him he can hear the bodies of wing-shot birds, dropping like stones out of the dark.

Out in front of the blind, wounded ducks are swimming in tiny circles. He thinks of excuses. He thinks he can explain himself away with terms like *delayed stress* or *teaching anxiety.* He is hunched now, leaning out of the gun port. Nothing left to do but put them in his game bag and bring them in, he thinks.

In the faintest light he wades out, gathers ducks, cradles them before he snaps their necks, placing each one gently in the game pouch behind his jacket, and then he tromps back to the blind, the light from the headlamp he wears twisting through the marsh. Just before he crawls into one of the upper bunks, he remembers what he's said to his farm-boy students every day for the past thirty years: "Don't you dinks dare waste a single grain of wood." And there in the weak light of his headlamp he can see perfectly how the backs of his hands are full of deep ridges, hardening veins, and holding them up to the light he whispers "teacher hands." And what he means is gray hands. Hands that rummage for chalk in the pockets of tweed blazers for a lifetime, a career in the minor leagues, he is fond of saying.

What he is thinking is that his hands have become the hands of a pussy. Useless. Hands that once killed men in the jungle with one surge or wielded a knife like it was made of air now reduced to writing lesson plans. He is thinking that his hands are limp appendages, the instinct rising in him to cut them off right there in the blind, while he is drunk enough to feel no pain. He would string them into a necklace and wear them home, walk into the woodshop and hold them near the ripping teeth of the radial arm saw and glare into the white faces of his boys.

In the darkness, he cradles his hands near his chest as if they were babies. If you snuck up on him now, in that weak light, you'd think he was dead or almost dead, weeping. And, backing out, you would hear the faint flutter of death somewhere off in the marsh grass, the night falling like black rain out of the sky.

Later, when the night had become so black you wouldn't be able to see your own finger in your nose, you could sit down near the blind and hear him muttering, sobbing, talking to himself, and then you'd hear the wild dogs coming in. Swamp mongrels, maybe ten or fifteen dogs, dropped off by their suburban owners, feral now, moving along the edge of the swamp. "Periphery," Houck would say to himself half in a stupor, half asleep, rising up firing again and again out of the black window toward their howling, the swamp alive, his head full of frenzy. Shooting into the dark, he could smell the odor of duck blood on his thumb, sighting into a black nothing, only sound, no lights for miles.

It's almost daylight now. Houck feels barely alive, his eyes sunken into his head. He squints through his right eye and holds his hands up to the faint light. He mutters to himself, almost singing, "Zip-A-Dee-Doo-Dah," a version from Nam he remembers, ending with "I'm gonna kill me a gook today." His voice trails off into a whisper while he pulls himself up to his knees, his chin resting on the sill.

He looks at his whitened knuckles, the tiny scars running like trap lines across both of his hands. VC scars: a month of being strung up by his fingers in the jungle. He remembers being cut down, his shoulders separated, aching for months.

Outside he checks his game bag: nothing. Only a few feathers, a leg or two. There are ducks floating around the blind, bits of wing and bills, their carcasses ravaged by the dogs. He stumbles through the knee-deep water, stuffing them into the bag. In ten minutes he's jammed twenty partial birds into the pouch and is on his way back through the marsh to the parking lot, his shotgun swinging across his back, mad now, not angry mad, but the kind of mad that drives you up and out of the place you're in. A madness brought on by monotony, a kind of ecstasy fueled by the smell of blood and loss. The need to get back home and once and for all set things up right.

But what he really needs is to cut his losses, start over. The need in him to clear out his head is like a taste in his mouth that won't go away. He turns around, retraces his steps, steps back into the blind, holds his lighter to the ceiling, and watches as the flames spread in a cloud of fire over his head. Twenty yards away and he's watching the last of the blind slump into the marsh; the hissing sound it makes when it hits the water is like the sound he remembers of napalm sifting through the trees, and then the smell of phosphorous burning underwater comes back to him, bits of skin being lifted off the arms of young children, their burning skin glowing in the dark.

The drive back north is a version of tag. He stalks cars and rides up on them and then blasts past, the drivers behind him flipping him off. Just outside Grayling he cuts off a guy driving a red Camaro, his tape player blasting a road tape of Bob Seger singing "Heavy Music" over and over, an endless loop, which is what Houck likes to think of as a perfect analogy for life, his life. He tells his boys every day that life is an endless series of repeated actions: "Get the actions down right, and you don't have to even think about taking a dump," he's said more than once. "Just put her on automatic, and get to a weekend."

By the time Houck pulls over, the guy from the Camaro is running toward the Jeep holding a pistol on him Miami-Vice style, and just as the man's face appears screaming at his window, Houck slides the shotgun up to the glass, motioning the guy closer, then pulls away, letting both barrels go, the glass spraying outward like a wave, in slow motion. On his way down the entry ramp Houck turns to look behind him and then hears the plink of six rounds from a .22 hitting his tailgate, the guy shouting and waving his fists. Only Houck is gone. "Nada," he says over and over. "Nada, nada, nada. You got nada, bucko," suppressing the urge to turn around and run the guy down, leave him for roadkill.

He doesn't go home but pulls up behind the school just after ten that night. In the dark he can make out the bus garage, illuminated by one mercury vapor lamp. He can barely see in through the tiny shop windows, the emergency exit sign glowing red over the single exit door.

He slips inside, leaves the lights off and heads for the

wood bunk, high from eight road beers and a hit of Jack
Daniels. He rearranges a few two-by-fours, slides a sheet
of marine plywood, the hull for Frank Dalton's rowboat
over the pile, then crawls in.

In the dim light of the sign, he can make out almost
everything in the shop. He crawls in and out a couple of
times, crawls to his office door to check his route, and
then moves back toward the blind he's made.

At home, well after midnight, he "checks his traps" as
he has come to call a kind of paying mindful attention
to all the snags in his life. He imagines walking through
the swamp near his house, pulling the steel leg traps
up from the murky water. Instead of muskrat, which is
what he's after, he imagines dark knots of trouble: affairs
through the years that went bad after only a week or two.
An "event" that lasted almost an entire school year with
one of the cheerleaders, years ago. He remembers how
he parked on a back road that first night after a football
game and slid his hands under her down jacket. Then the
elaborate methods he'd used to arrange secret meetings:
calling her house to talk to her older sister on the outside
chance she might answer. The height of it meant chap-
eroning the senior trip to Cedar Point, and how they had
managed to sneak into a room together for the night. He
marked the special spot on his desk where he made love
to her during her lunch hour for weeks on end, the spot
now covered by a huge desk blotter, only the memory of
her loose in his bloodstream, as if she were some kind

of particle, diminished, but still hanging around. "Like ether," he'd mumble to himself sometimes when he lifted the planning calendar and ran his fingers over the spot she had graced so many times. Finally, after her parents found out, he had to back her father off with a pistol in the faculty parking lot. Later, there was pleading, lots of bargaining with the superintendent, but he kept his job and "kept his nose clean," as he liked to say, running his forefinger under his nose, "but not this," he'd say to his few friends who knew but would never rat.

Daylight. Back to work. The smell of shotgun shells is still on his hands. All that firing. The blind in shambles a day ago and 250 miles below him. Houck moves toward the kitchen, drinks a beer and pulls on his work clothes: a pair of khakis and a blue Sears work shirt, long wool socks and his jungle boots. Once at school he slips in the back way and waits in his office. First hour. Independent study in woodshop for three boys who can't make it in the regular class. Court referrals. Farm boys with an attitude. He can hear them coming through the door. On his notepad he writes: day 5,389. Lesson: survive or die, not bookcases or tables. He's not planning on getting the boys in a circle to tell them how to router a table top or how to mitre-cut a picture frame. No dado talk today, he mumbles. Just survive or die.

Before he lifts a single slat in his office blind with his thumb like he always does, he knows exactly what he'll see: three farm boys cutting and sawing. "Making kindling," he's thinking. Then he hits the main power switch, and the lights flicker awhile then die. He hears Frank Patterson shouting, "Turn the goddamn lights on!" From across the shop Ed Farrel tells him to keep sawing: "Only a pussy would stop. There's enough light coming in from the window, so keep cutting, you pussy."

In the half-dark Houck is crawling along the floor. He stops at Frank Patterson's feet and slides like a snake up his back. In one motion he grabs his crotch with his right hand and covers his mouth with his left. "Don't make a sound, Frankie," he whispers into his ear. "Move with me. Move slow. Move quiet, you little fuck."

Together, they crawl under the tables, toward the makeshift blind in the corner. Houck wraps his feet and hands, gags his mouth, and then sticks his face into the boy's. "Don't move. I'll be back," he whispers.

Two more boys cutting and laughing in a dark wood-shop, Houck is thinking. Easy prey. Both of them go down as if they were made of paper, Houck almost conjuring himself between the machines and tables as if he were air. He takes both boys the same way, and then all three are sitting in front of him in the blind. They start shaking visibly when Houck pulls out his combat knife.

One by one he slides the edge up close to their faces and then cuts the air between them. "If this were jungle, you'd all be dead. Thirty years I've been at this, and you're the worst excuses for flesh I've ever seen. People like you don't last long out there. It's alcohol or car wrecks, prison. You're losers. Always will be, but remember this. In the jungle you'd all be dead." Houck uses his knife to cut through the tape. "Now get outta here."

He is pushing them out the door, and just as Frank Patterson is about to flip him the bird, Houck pulls the knife from its sheath. "Not today Frank," he says, "not tomorrow, not the day after tomorrow. Go find some brains."

Before he locks the door, George Houck takes out a Zippo, one he'd gotten from Steve House. A "'Nam lighter," given away in Khe Sanh during the seige. Traded, really, for a pack of smokes and a candy bar. He spreads some cleaning fluid on his desk and lights a corner of his grade book. "Adios, motherfuckers," he says under his breath. In the parking lot he can hear the second-hour bell. And he can hear Frank Patterson driving back through the woods in his old Chevy pickup, the heavy thump of his sub-woofers pounding through the trees. Houck waits until he hears the fire alarms go off and then sees students piling out into the parking lot at the north end of the school.

He looks back into the cargo area of his Jeep: he's got his life there. Literally. A sleeping bag. A couple of guns. Some clothes and a few cans of food. He locks up the four-wheel drive, hits the tape deck, and wheels a U-ie.

He hits fifty by the time he's close to the school. He can see a small wisp of smoke coming from the roof. And right there, in a parking lot where he once pulled Margaret Scheer's jeans off after a basketball game, he feels something let go. He hears ducks, he thinks. The sound of a shotgun going off in his head. He imagines himself reaching down into a bag of snakes, a neck going soft, limp, dead in his hands.

He wants to go north. Wants to just drive and think of how Frank Patterson and Ed Ferrel and Jerry Bolster will tell it to their friends. And how they'll get it all wrong describing how the knife flashed in front of their faces. They'll say they weren't scared, but Houck had smelled the shit in their pants, had seen how their eyes gave no hint. No notion of what they'd been taught in such a short time. No reflection of what it meant to be so close to being dead.